SPECTRUM®

Critical Thinking for Math

Grade 2

Published by Spectrum®
an imprint of Carson Dellosa Education
Greensboro, NC

Spectrum®
An imprint of Carson Dellosa Education
P.O. Box 35665
Greensboro, NC 27425 USA

ISBN 978-1-4838-3549-5

03-053217784

Table of Contents Grade 2

Table of Contents, continued

Check What You Know

Understanding and Using Numbers

Draw an array to show each equation. Then, solve the equation.

1. $1 + 1 + 1 =$ _____

2. $2 + 2 =$ _____

3. Count by 10s. Write the missing numbers.

   20, _____, _____, _____, _____

4. Count by 5s. Write the missing numbers.

   55, _____, _____, _____, _____

5. Count by 2s. Write the missing numbers.

   74, _____, _____, _____, _____

Draw a picture to decide if the number is even or odd. Write **even** or **odd** on the line.

6. **16**

7. **13**

_____

_____

Lesson 1.1　Grouping Objects

You can draw an array to help you write and solve equations. The apples below are in an array with 2 rows of 3 apples. So, 3 + 3 = 6.

$$\underline{3} + \underline{3} = \underline{6}$$

Draw an array to show each equation. Then, solve the equation.

4 + 4 + 4 = _____

1 + 1 + 1 + 1 + 1 = _____

5 + 5 + 5 + 5 = _____

Lesson 1.1 Grouping Objects

Draw an array to show each equation. Then, solve the equation.

4 + 4 = _____

4 + 4 + 4 + 4 = _____

5 + 5 + 5 = _____

3 + 3 + 3 + 3 + 3 = _____

Lesson 1.2 Skip Counting

To skip count, take the amount you are skip counting by and add on to the previous number.

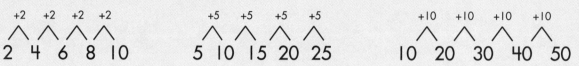

Count by 2. Write the missing numbers.

20, _____, _____, _____, 28, _____, _____, _____, 36

Count by 5. Write the missing numbers.

35, _____, _____, _____, 55, _____, _____, _____, 75

Count by 10. Write the missing numbers.

_____, _____, _____, 60, _____, _____, _____, 100

Lesson 1.2 Skip Counting

Start at 12. Count by 2s. Write as many numbers as you can.

Start at 45. Count by 5s. Write as many numbers as you can.

Start at 20. Count by 10s. Write as many numbers as you can.

Lesson 1.3 Even or Odd?

Eight is an even number because 8 pieces of pizza can be **evenly** split between 2. Both sides will get 4 pieces of pizza.

Five is an odd number because 5 bananas cannot be **evenly** split between 2. Both sides will **not** get the same number.

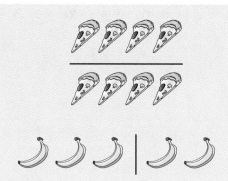

Draw a picture to help you decide if the given number is even or odd. Write **even** or **odd** on the line.

8 _____

3 _____

7 _____

Lesson 1.3 Even or Odd?

Draw a picture to help you decide if the given number is even or odd. Write **even** or **odd** on the line.

10 _____

5 _____

15 _____

20 _____

Check What You Learned

Understanding and Using Numbers

Draw an array to show each equation. Then, solve the equation. Decide if each total is even or odd. Circle **even** or **odd**.

1. 5 + 5 + 5 =

Total: _____

Even or Odd

2. 2 + 2 + 2 + 2 + 2 =

Total: _____

Even or Odd

Write the equation to match each array. Then, solve the equation. Count by the number given to find the next 4 numbers.

3.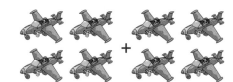

_____ + _____ = _____

Count by 4s.
Next 4 numbers: _____, _____,

_____, _____

4.

_____ + _____ = _____

Count by 2s.
Next 4 numbers: _____, _____,

_____, _____

CHAPTER 1 POSTTEST

Check What You Know

Addition and Subtraction Through 20

Add or subtract. Draw models to show your thinking.

1. 16 – 10 = _____

2. 18 – 9 = _____

Add or subtract. Draw a number line to show your thinking.

3. 17 – _____ = 15

4. 20 – 3 = _____

Solve. Draw models to show your thinking.

5. Brittany's horse eats 20 apples a day. She has 12 apples at her house. Lynn brings over 7 more apples. Will the girls have enough apples to feed the horse for the day? Why or why not?

Lesson 2.1   Drawing a Picture to Add

You can draw a picture to help you solve an addition problem.

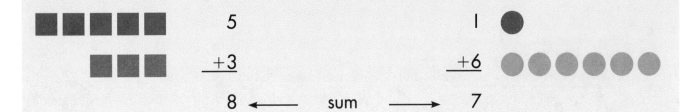

Add. Draw a picture to show your thinking.

7
+ 4
____

9
+
____
18

Write 2 different addition problems that each have a total of 19. Draw pictures to show the problems.

Lesson 2.2 Drawing a Picture to Subtract

You can draw a picture to help you solve a subtraction problem.

Subtract. Draw a picture to show your thinking.

8 − 6 = _____

12 − _____ = 4

Anthony blows up 18 balloons for a birthday party. 4 of the balloons pop. When the party is over, there are only 5 balloons left. How many more balloons popped during the party?

Lesson 2.3 Using a Number Line to Add

You can use a number line to add. Start at one addend, and count on the number line using the other addend. The number you stop on is your answer.

12 + 4 = _____

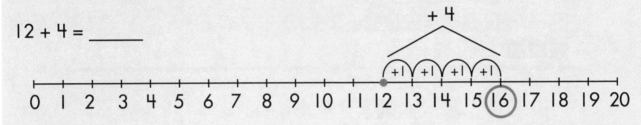

Add. Use a number line to show your thinking.

5 + 2 = _____

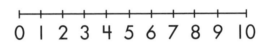

8 + 3 = _____

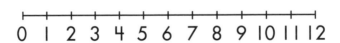

Bonnie uses 2 tissue paper rolls to make decorative flowers. She uses 4 feet of the yellow tissue paper roll and 9 feet of the pink tissue paper roll. How many feet of tissue paper roll did Bonnie use?

Lesson 2.4   Using a Number Line to Subtract

You can use a number line to solve subtraction problems. Start at the number you are subtracting from. Count down by the amount you are subtracting. The number you stop on is your answer.

17 − 7 = _____

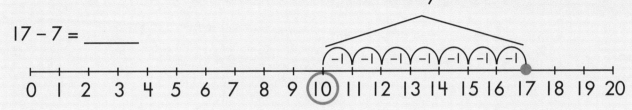

Subtract. Use a number line to show your thinking.

20 − 5 = _____

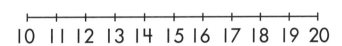

14 − 6 = _____

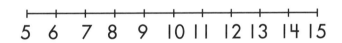

Deanna has 16 crayons. She gives 5 crayons to her little sister. How many crayons does Deanna have left?

Lesson 2.5 Solving Problems by Adding On

You can solve addition problems by using the strategy of adding on.

$11 + 4 = ?$

+4

1 2 3 4 5 6 7 8 9 10 11 12 13 14 15

Start at 11 and count on 4 more.

$11 + 4 = 15$

Add. Use the strategy of adding on.

$15 + 2 =$ _____

$9 + 8 =$ _____

Reid was collecting bottles to recycle. His goal for the week was to collect 20 bottles. On Sunday, Monday, and Tuesday, he collected a total of 6 bottles. On Wednesday, Thursday, Friday, and Saturday he collected a total of 9 bottles. Did Reid meet his goal for the week? If not, how many more bottles does he need?

Lesson 2.6 Using Addition for Subtraction

You can use addition to solve subtraction problems.

15 − 6 = ?   Think: 6 + ? = 15.

Use strategies such as counting on, drawing a picture, or using a number line to solve the addition problem.

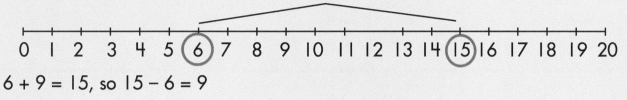

6 + 9 = 15, so 15 − 6 = 9

Solve. Use addition to help you show your thinking.

Mr. Chadwick has 18 fish in his aquarium. 8 of the fish are catfish. The others are zebrafish. Explain how you can figure out how many of the fish are zebrafish by using addition.

Next week, Mr. Chadwick will have 25 living things in his aquarium after he adds plants and snails. Write a subtraction sentence to show how many plants and snails Mr. Chadwick will add to the aquarium.

Lesson 2.7   Addition and Subtraction

Add or subtract. Use any of the strategies mentioned previously to show your thinking.

$5 + 9 =$ _____

_____

$12 +$ _____ $= 17$

_____

_____ $+ 7 = 14$

_____

Write 3 different problems that each have an answer of 13.

NAME _____

Lesson 2.8 Adding and Subtracting in the Real World

Erika caught 8 fish at the pond. April caught 12 more fish. They decided to put 5 fish back. How many fish did Erika and April take home?

First, find how many fish they caught altogether.

8 + 12 = ?

Next, solve to find how many fish Erika and April got to take home.

20 – 5 = ?

Erika and April got to take home 15 fish.

Solve the problem. Draw pictures to show your thinking.

Ivy made 10 cupcakes for the bake sale. Hannah made 10 chocolate-covered pretzels. On the way to the sale, 2 pretzels broke and 1 cupcake fell on the ground. How many baked goods do the girls have to sell now?

Spectrum Critical Thinking for Math
Grade 2

Lesson 2.8
Adding and Subtracting in the Real World
21

Lesson 2.8   Adding and Subtracting in the Real World

Solve the problems. Show your work.

The toy store has 18 toy cars left in stock. On Monday, it sells 8 of the cars. On Tuesday, it sells 3 more of the cars. On Wednesday, Mark comes to the store and wants to buy a toy car. Are there any left for Mark to buy? Use a number line to show your thinking.

Paige wants to plant flowers in her yard. She picks out 12 red tulips and 7 yellow daffodils at the store. If she buys 20 flowers today, she will get a discount. Will Paige get a discount with the number of flowers she chose? Draw pictures to show your thinking.

Brad has some books about sports on his bookshelf. Joey has 4 books about football on his bookshelf. Altogether, they have 15 books about sports. How many books does Brad have? Draw pictures to show your thinking.

Check What You Learned

Addition and Subtraction Through 20

1. Solve. Draw pictures to show your thinking.

Nathan had 15 baseball caps. He sold some of the caps to earn money for a new baseball bat. After his sale, he had 3 baseball caps left. How many baseball caps did Nathan sell? Then, Nathan's grandmother visited and gave him 2 brand-new baseball caps. How many baseball caps does Nathan have now?

2. Solve. Use a number line to show your thinking.

Samantha bakes some key lime pies to sell at the bake sale. Taylor bakes 11 peanut butter pies to sell at the bake sale. They have 15 total pies. How many key lime pies did Samantha make?

3. Add. Use the strategy of adding on.

$8 + 7 =$ _____

CHAPTER 2 POSTTEST

Check What You Know

Addition and Subtraction with 2-Digit Numbers

Solve. Draw pictures to show your thinking.

1. 12 + 27 = _____

2. 49 – 48 = _____

Solve. Use a number line to show your thinking.

3. 10 + 30 = _____

4. 84 – 71 = _____

Solve the problem. Draw pictures to show your thinking.

5. Westberg's Pizza Shop sells pizza by the slice. On Monday, it sold 37 slices. On Tuesday, it sold 50 slices. The goal for the week was 99 slices. Do you think the shop will meet its goal? Why or why not?

Lesson 3.1 Adding with Tens and Ones Blocks

You can use tens and ones blocks to help you solve a problem.

$$\begin{array}{r} 25 \\ + 43 \\ \hline \end{array}$$

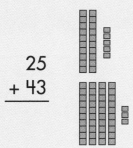

Add the ones. 8 ones
Add the tens. 6 tens
25 + 43 = 68

Add. Draw tens and ones blocks to show your thinking.

$$\begin{array}{r} 36 \\ + 43 \\ \hline \end{array}$$

Write the problem for the tens and ones blocks shown.

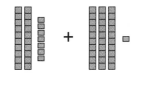

_____ + _____ = _____

Draw another way to show this problem with tens and ones blocks.

Lesson 3.2 Subtracting with Tens and Ones Blocks

You can draw tens and ones blocks to help you subtract.

$$\begin{array}{r} 77 \\ -\,26 \\ \hline \end{array}$$

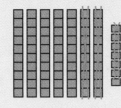

There are 5 tens and 1 one left.
So, the answer is 51.

Subtract. Draw tens and ones blocks to show your thinking.

$$\begin{array}{r} 49 \\ -\,39 \\ \hline \end{array}$$

Using tens and ones blocks, write a subtraction problem with an answer of 21. Write a word problem to go with the subtraction problem.

_____

_____

_____

Lesson 3.3 Using a Number Line to Add

You can add 2-digit numbers using a number line. Break the second addend into tens and ones.

40 + 34 = ?

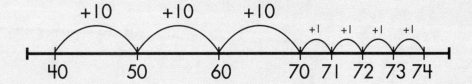

40 + 34 = 74

Add. Use a number line to show your thinking.

66
+ 22
———

Charlotte had 34 bean plants. Mika had 53 bean plants. Then, Charlotte and Mika were given 13 more plants by a neighbor. How many plants do they have now?

Lesson 3.4   Using a Number Line to Subtract

You can subtract 2-digit numbers using a number line.

82 − 51 = ?

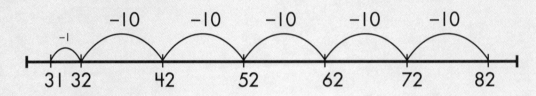

82 − 51 = 31

Subtract. Use a number line to show your thinking.

36 − 24 =

Write the subtraction problem for the number line given.

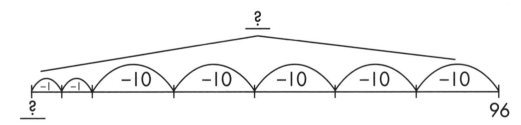

_____ − _____ = _____

Lesson 3.5   Finding Missing Numbers

You can use different strategies to find a missing addend in an addition problem:
42 + _____ = 97.
Begin with the largest number in the problem. Subtract the smaller number to find the missing value.

Draw a picture.

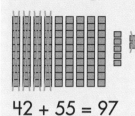

42 + 55 = 97

Use a number line.

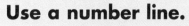

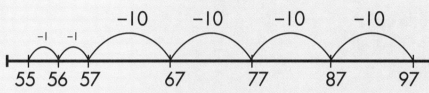

Solve. Draw a picture or number line to show your thinking.

Upton went to the grocery store. He bought a banana for 35 cents. He also bought a melon. He spent 83 cents total. How much did Upton spend on the melon?

Brooke went to the grocery store and bought an apple for 20 cents. She also bought an orange. She spent 53 cents total. How much did Brooke spend on the orange?

Lesson 3.5   Finding Missing Numbers

You can use different strategies to find a missing number in a subtraction problem: 69 – _____ = 44.
Begin with the largest number in the problem. Subtract the smaller number to find the missing value.

Draw a picture.   **Use a number line.**

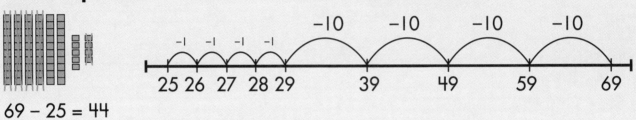

69 – 25 = 44

Subtract. Draw a picture or number line to show your thinking.

Connor buys a crayon and a pen for 99 cents. The pen costs 65 cents. How much does the crayon cost?

Lesson 3.6   Adding and Subtracting in the Real World

You can solve word problems using strategies such as drawing a picture, using a number line, or writing an equation.

There were 28 dogs in the dog park on Saturday. Some dogs left the park. There are 14 dogs remaining. How many dogs left?

Write an equation.

$28 - ? = 14$ $28 - 14 = 14$

14 dogs left the dog park.

Use a number line.

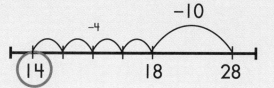

Draw a picture.

Solve the problem with a number line and with blocks.

Derek finds 23 frogs at the pond, but 12 hop away. Justin finds 29 frogs at the lake, but 21 hop away. How many frogs do Derek and Justin have?

Lesson 3.6 Adding and Subtracting in the Real World

Solve the problems. Show your answer using both a number line and tens and ones blocks.

Murphy Elementary School had 88 cartons of milk on Monday. After breakfast, there were 25 cartons left in the cooler. How many cartons of milk did the school serve for breakfast?

On Monday, Mr. Novak sold 16 lawnmowers at his hardware store. At the end of the week, he had sold 48 lawnmowers. How many lawnmowers did Mr. Novak sell after Monday?

Lesson 3.7   Addition with Renaming

You can draw tens and ones blocks to help you add 2-digit numbers.

$$\begin{array}{r} 36 \\ + 45 \\ \hline \end{array}$$ = 81

Count the ones.
Trade in 10 ones for a tens block.
Count the tens and the ones left over.

Add. Draw tens and ones blocks to show your thinking.

Jimmy runs a lemonade stand at the end of his driveway for 4 weeks during the summer. The table shows how much he made each week.

Week 1	$24
Week 2	$29
Week 3	$28
Week 4	$27

How much money did Jimmy make altogether in Week 1 and Week 2?

Lesson 3.7   Addition with Renaming

You can use a number line to help you add 2-digit numbers.

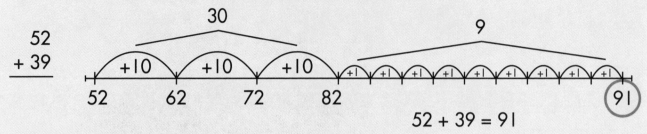

52
+ 39
_____

$52 + 39 = 91$

Start your number line at the first number given (52).
Using tens, count forward by the number of tens you are adding (30).
Using ones, count forward by the number of ones you are adding (9).
The number you land on is the answer.

Add. Use a number line to show your thinking.

$32 + 49 =$

Write the number sentence for the problem shown on the number line.

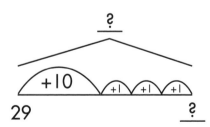

_____ + _____ = _____

Lesson 3.8 Subtraction with Renaming

You can draw tens and ones blocks to help you subtract 2-digit numbers.

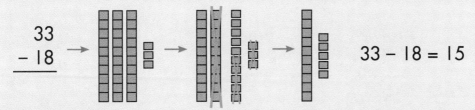

$$33 - 18 = 15$$

Take away the ones. You will need to break up a tens block.
Go to the tens. Cross out the 1 ten you are subtracting.
Count the tens and ones blocks you have left.

Subtract. Draw tens and ones blocks to show your thinking.

62 birds are perching in the big oak tree. 29 birds fly away. How many birds are left in the tree?

Another 14 birds fly away. How many are left in the tree now?

Lesson 3.8 Subtraction with Renaming

You can subtract 2-digit numbers using a number line.

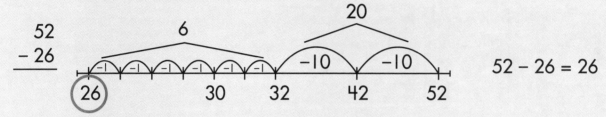

$$52 - 26 = 26$$

Start your number line with the first number given.
Using tens, count backward by the number of tens you are subtracting (20).
Using ones, count backward by the number of ones you are subtracting (6).
The number you land on is the answer (26).

Subtract. Use a number line to show your work.

Becky and Tina go on a nature walk. Becky finds 33 snails. Tina finds 28 snails. How many more snails does Becky find than Tina?

If 2 of Becky's snails slither away, how does that change your answer?

Lesson 3.9 Renaming in the Real World

Solve the problems.

Scott has 31 toy cars. He gives some of them to a friend. Now he has only 15 toy cars. How may toy cars did Scott give to his friend? Draw tens and ones blocks to show your thinking.

Rachel's class collects 38 cans of food for the food drive. Wesley's class collects 45 cans of food. The goal for the 2 classes is to collect 80 cans of food. Did the classes meet their goal? Draw a number line to show your thinking.

Lesson 3.9 Renaming in the Real World

Write a word problem to go with the subtraction problem. Solve the problem by drawing a number line.

65 – 39 =

_____

_____

_____

_____

_____

_____

_____

_____

Check What You Learned

Addition and Subtraction with 2-Digit Numbers

1. Add or subtract. Draw models to show your thinking.

   Caitlyn has $87 in her piggy bank. She buys a new dress for $55. How much money does she have left? Use tens and ones blocks to show your thinking.

2. Add or subtract. Use a number line to show your thinking.

   Caitlyn wants to buy a new pair of sandals that costs $47. How much more money will she need? Use a number line to show your thinking.

3. Write the number sentence that goes with the number line shown below. Then, show the problem using tens and ones blocks.

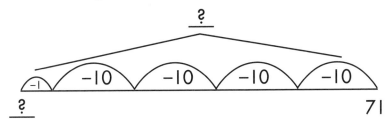

Mid-Test Chapters 1-3

Draw an array to show each equation. Then, solve the equation. Show if each total is even or odd by circling **even** or **odd**.

1. 3 + 3 + 3 + 3 =

Total: _____

Even or Odd

2. 5 + 5 + 5 =

Total: _____

Even or Odd

Write the equation to match each array. Then, solve the equation. Count by the amount given to find the next 4 numbers.

3.

_____ + _____ + _____ = _____

Count by 7s.
Next 4 numbers: _____, _____,

_____, _____

4.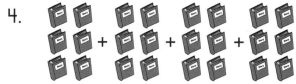

_____ + _____ + _____ + _____

= _____

Count by 6s.
Next 4 numbers: _____, _____,

_____, _____

Mid-Test Chapters 1-3

Solve the problems.

5. On Saturday, Michelle found 9 sand dollars at the beach. On Sunday, she found 4 more sand dollars. On her way home from the beach, 7 of the sand dollars broke. How many sand dollars does Michelle have left? Draw a picture to show your thinking.

6. Logan needs 15 rubber bands to finish making his rubber band ball. He finds 7 after school. How many more rubber bands does he need to finish? Draw a picture to show your thinking.

7. Write the equation for the models shown below. Then, draw the problem on a number line.

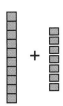

Mid-Test Chapters 1-3

Solve the problems. Draw pictures to show your thinking.

8. At the county fair, children can play games and earn tickets for prizes. Shelby wants the large teddy bear that costs 100 tickets. She has 36 tickets. How many more tickets does she need?

9. Shelby's brother gives her 25 of his tickets. Can she get the bear now?

Solve the problems. Use a number line to show your thinking.

10. William and Tyler each have 24 pennies. Denise has 31 pennies. How many pennies do William and Tyler have in all?

11. How many pennies do all 3 children have in all?

Check What You Know

Working with 3-Digit Numbers

Complete problems 1– 3 with the number **437**.

1. Show the number in expanded form.

_____

2. Show the number in number name form.

_____

3. Skip count backward by 2s to show the next 4 numbers.

_____, _____, _____, _____

4. Use a number line to compare:

847 _____ 625

Check What You Know

CHAPTER 4 PRETEST

Working with 3-Digit Numbers

5. Add. Use a number line to show your thinking.

641 + 208 =

6. Subtract. Use blocks to show your thinking.

181 – 57 =

7. Solve the problem. Use a number line to show your work.

Abigail collected 155 bottle caps to make jewelry. When she got home from school, she noticed that she only had 60 bottle caps in her kit. How many bottle caps did Abigail lose? She needs 100 bottle caps to make a necklace and a bracelet. How many more bottle caps does she need to be able to make the necklace and bracelet?

Lesson 4.1 Counting and Writing 3-Digit Numbers

You can show 3-digit numbers like 253 in different ways.

Hundreds, Tens, and Ones Blocks:

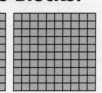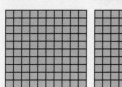

Expanded Form:

200 + 50 + 3

Number Name:

two hundred fifty-three

Draw the number given using blocks. Write the expanded form of each number.

167

_____ + _____ + _____ = _____

651

_____ + _____ + _____ = _____

NAME _____

Lesson 4.1 Counting and Writing 3-Digit Numbers

Draw the number given using blocks. Write the number name of each number.

214

_____

463

_____

908

Lesson 4.2   Skip Counting with 3-Digit Numbers

Start at each number given. Skip count by the number given. Write as many numbers as you can.

1. Start at 200. Count by 10s.

_____

_____

_____

2. Start at 532. Count by 2s.

_____

_____

_____

3. Start at 300. Count backward by 5s.

_____

_____

_____

4. Start at 100. Count by 100s.

_____

_____

_____

Lesson 4.3   Comparing 3-Digit Numbers

To compare 3-digit numbers, break each number down into hundreds, tens, and ones blocks. Then, tell which number has more blocks.

   503 _____ 362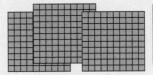

503 has more blocks, therefore 503 is greater than 362. **503 > 362**

Break each number down into hundreds, tens, and ones blocks. Determine which number is greater. Write **>**, **<**, or **=** on the line.

567 _____ 564

354 _____ 453

Lesson 4.3   Comparing 3-Digit Numbers

When comparing 3-digit numbers, you can use a number line to help you tell which number is greater and which one is smaller.

122 _____ 245

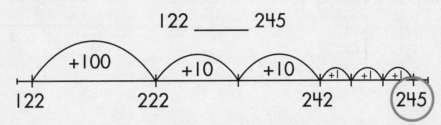

The number to the left on the number line is always less than the number on the right. Therefore, 122 is less than 245. **122 < 245**

Show each number given on a number line. Determine which number is greater. Write **>**, **<**, or **=** on the line.

148 _____ 369

959 _____ 767

Lesson 4.4 Adding 3-Digit Numbers

You can combine hundreds, tens, and ones blocks to help you add 3-digit numbers.

$$188 + 365$$

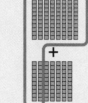 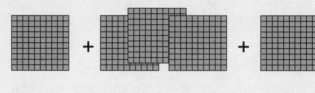

First, combine ones: 8 + 5. You can trade 10 ones for 1 ten.
Next, combine tens: 8 + 6 + 1. You can trade 10 tens for 1 hundred.
Last, combine hundreds: 1 + 3 + 1.
Count the blocks you have left to find your answer. **188 + 365 = 553**

Solve the problem. Use hundreds, tens, and ones blocks to show your thinking.

2 months ago, a restaurant sold 239 orders of bacon cheese fries. Last month, it sold 111 orders of bacon cheese fries. If the restaurant sells more than 350 orders in 3 months, the fries will stay on the menu. How many orders does the restaurant have to sell this month for the item to stay on the menu? How do you know?

Lesson 4.4 Adding 3-Digit Numbers

You can use a number line to solve addition problems with 3-digit numbers.

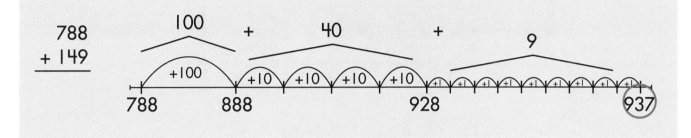

$$788 + 149$$

Add. Use a number line to show your thinking.

203 + 299 =

338 + 187 =

Lesson 4.5 Subtracting 3-Digit Numbers

You can use models to help you subtract 3-digit numbers.

486
– 109

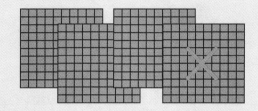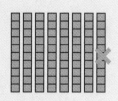

Start with the ones. You cannot subtract 9 from 6, so borrow a ten.
Now, you can subtract: $16 - 9 = 7$.
Next, go to the tens. Since you borrowed a ten, you now have 7 tens. $7 - 0$ is 7.
Last, subtract hundreds: $4 - 1 = 3$. **486 – 109 = 377**

Solve the problem. Use models to show your thinking.

Lola has $543 in her bank account. She wants to spend $457 on a new computer. After she buys the computer, how much money will Lola have left? Will she have enough money to buy a web camera that costs $38 and a computer game that costs $29? Will she have any money left over?

Lesson 4.5 Subtracting 3-Digit Numbers

You can use a number line to subtract 3-digit numbers.

519
− 120

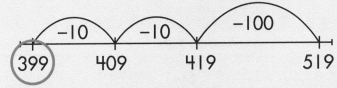

Start your number line with the number you are subtracting from.
First, count backward by the hundreds (100).
Next, count backward by the tens (20).
Last, count backward by the ones (0).
The number you land on is your answer. **519 − 120 = 399**

Subtract. Use a number line to show your thinking.

710 − 447 =

Write the subtraction problem shown on the number line.

_____ − _____ = _____

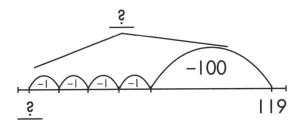

Lesson 4.6   Creating 3-Digit Problems

The answer is:	The questions might be:
675	553 + 122
	794 − 119
	230 + 445

Write 3 problems for each answer given.

812

305

664

Lesson 4.7　3-Digit Numbers in the Real World

Yasmin collected 325 bottle caps for her art project. Her school donated 299 more bottle caps. Yasmin needs 800 bottle caps to complete her project. Will she have enough to complete her project? If not, how many more bottle caps does she need?

First, you must determine how many bottle caps she has: 325 + 299 = 624. Now, you know she does **not** have enough bottle caps because 624 < 800. To find out how many more bottle caps she needs you must subtract: 800 − 624 = 176. Yasmin needs 176 more bottle caps to finish her art project.

Solve the problem. Explain your thinking.

Roxanne makes jewelry to sell at craft fairs. She has 251 red beads and 439 blue beads in her kit. To be successful at her next craft fair, she needs 900 of each color bead. How many more red beads does she need to buy?

How many more blue beads does she need to buy?

How many total beads does she need to buy before her next craft fair?

Lesson 4.7   3-Digit Numbers in the Real World

Write a word problem to go with each addition or subtraction problem.
Then, solve each problem.

411 + 120 =

_____

_____

_____

_____

719 – 532 =

_____

_____

_____

_____

Check What You Learned

Working with 3-Digit Numbers

Complete the following with the number **674**.

1. Show the number in hundreds, tens, and ones blocks.

2. Show the number in expanded form.

_____

3. Show the number in number name form.

_____

4. Skip count by 100s to show the next 4 numbers.

_____, _____, _____, _____

5. Skip count backward by 5s to show the next 4 numbers.

_____, _____, _____, _____

6. Skip count by 10s to show the next 4 numbers.

_____, _____, _____, _____

Check What You Learned

Working with 3-Digit Numbers

Compare: 226 _____ 298

7. Use blocks.

8. Use a number line.

9. Solve the problem. Use blocks and a number line to show your thinking.

   203 + 211 =

Check What You Know

Measurement

1. Melissa got home from swimming at 3:00 P.M. It takes her 20 minutes to walk home. What time did Melissa leave the pool? Show the time on both clocks below.

2. Estimate the length of each object. Then, use a ruler to measure each object in inches and centimeters.

Estimate: _____ in. _____ cm   Estimate: _____ in. _____ cm

Actual: _____ in. _____ cm   Actual: _____ in. _____ cm

3. Create a line plot based on the following data.
   4 in., 7 in., 2 in., 3 in., 4 in., 4 in., 5 in., 7 in., 2 in., 2 in., 3 in., 4 in.

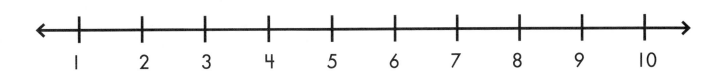

NAME _____

Check What You Know

Measurement

Favorite Ice Cream Flavors

Mint Chocolate Chip	🍦🍦🍦🍦🍦🍦🍦
Peanut Butter Cup	🍦🍦🍦🍦🍦🍦🍦🍦🍦🍦
Cookies and Cream	🍦🍦🍦🍦🍦🍦🍦🍦

🍦 = 1 person

4. Use the information in the picture graph to create a bar graph below.

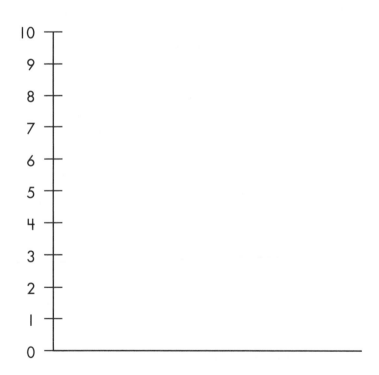

Use the graphs to answer the questions.

5. How many people were polled to create these graphs?

_____

6. How many more people liked peanut butter cup and mint chocolate chip than cookies and cream?

_____

7. How many more people should be polled to make it so 30 people voted?

_____

Lesson 5.1   Time to the Hour and Half Hour

Write sentences to go with the pictures. Tell the time shown.

The children play ball in the park at 11:00 A.M.

Write sentences to go with the pictures. Tell the time shown.

_____

_____

_____

Lesson 5.2   Time to the Quarter Hour

These clocks tell the time.

The time is eight fifteen.

The time is two forty-five.

Read the story. Then, answer the questions. Show the time on each clock.

Today is the day Andrew goes on his first airplane ride! He needs to arrive at the airport by 5:45 A.M. Once he gets to the airport, he must check in by 6:15 A.M. Andrew will start boarding the plane 15 minutes later. Once the plane takes off, Andrew can relax. The plane will land at 1:45 P.M. Andrew is so excited for his first flight!

What time does Andrew have to get to the airport?

What time does Andrew have to check in?

What time will Andrew start boarding the plane?

What time does Andrew's plane land?

Lesson 5.3 Time in the Real World

Each number on the clock represents 5 minutes of time.

From 12 to 1 is 5 minutes.
From 12 to 3 is 15 minutes.
From 12 to 6 is 30 minutes.
From 12 to 9 is 45 minutes.
From 12 to 12 is 60 minutes (1 hour).

Solve. Write the time on each clock given.

Kennedy went for a walk at 4:30 P.M. She walked 15 minutes down the road. What time did Kennedy stop walking?

Frederico turned off the television at 6:00 P.M. He had watched TV for 25 minutes before he turned it off. What time did Frederico start watching TV?

Lesson 5.4 Estimating Inches

To estimate the length of an object, use what you already know about measurement to make your best guess at how long the object is. The word **about** is used to describe how long the object might be.

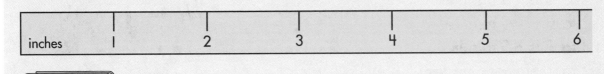

The paper clip is about 1 inch long.

Use the ruler above to estimate how many inches long each object is.

about _____ inches

about _____ inches

about _____ inches

Lesson 5.5 Estimating Centimeters

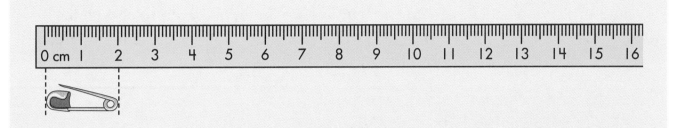

The safety pin is about 2 centimeters long.

Use the ruler above to estimate how many centimeters long each object is.

about _____ centimeters

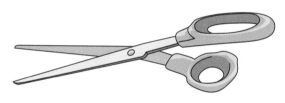

about _____ centimeters

about _____ centimeters

Lesson 5.6   Measuring Inches

To measure an object to the nearest inch, line up the edge of the ruler with the end of the object you are measuring. Look to the right. To determine the nearest inch, look to see what number the right end is closest to.

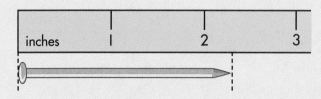

To the nearest inch, the nail is 2 inches long.

Choose 5 different writing tools (pen, pencil, crayon, marker, highlighter, etc.). Use a ruler to measure each tool to the nearest inch. Write the name and length of the tool on the lines below.

1. _____   _____ inch(es)

2. _____   _____ inch(es)

3. _____   _____ inch(es)

4. _____   _____ inch(es)

5. _____   _____ inch(es)

Lesson 5.7   Measuring Centimeters

Measure centimeters the same way you measure inches.

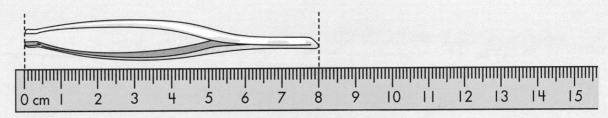

The tweezers are 8 centimeters long.

Use a ruler to measure each object in centimeters.

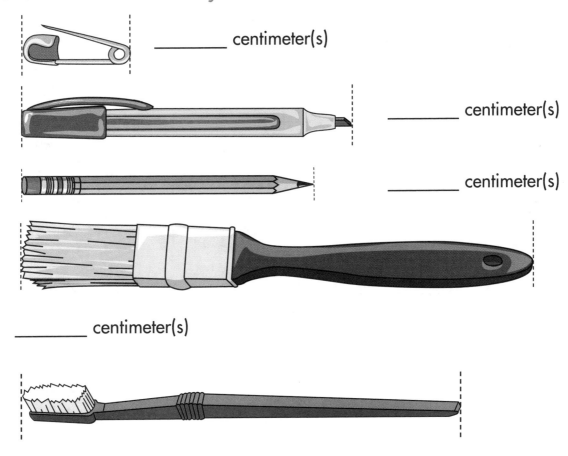

_____ centimeter(s)

_____ centimeter(s)

_____ centimeter(s)

_____ centimeter(s)

_____ centimeter(s)

Lesson 5.8   Comparing Measurements

You can compare measurements in inches and centimeters.

The toothbrush is 12 centimeters long.
The toothbrush is about 5 inches long.

Choose 5 eating utensils (fork, spoon, knife, chopstick, spork, etc.). Ask an adult to help you with any sharp utensils! Use a ruler to measure each in centimeters. Then, measure again to the nearest inch. Write the name of the utensil and how long it is on the lines below.

1. _____ _____ inches _____ centimeters

2. _____ _____ inches _____ centimeters

3. _____ _____ inches _____ centimeters

4. _____ _____ inches _____ centimeters

5. _____ _____ inches _____ centimeters

What do you notice about the measurements in centimeters compared to those in inches? What explains this?

_____

_____

_____

Lesson 5.9   Measurement in the Real World

You can use a number line to help you solve word problems involving lengths.

Becca wants to make a 28-inch necklace out of ribbon. She has a piece of ribbon that is 45 inches long. How many inches does Becca need to cut off in order to make her necklace the correct length?

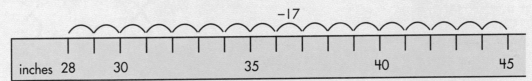

Start at 45 and count backward until you reach 28.
The number you counted is the amount Becca needs to cut off: 17 inches.

Solve. Use a number line to show your work.

Blake lines up 4 of her pencils and measures them. The total length of Blake's pencils is 60 centimeters. Delinda lines up 3 of her pencils and measures them. The total length of Delinda's pencils is 30 centimeters. What is the total length of all of Blake and Delinda's pencils?

Lesson 5.10 Making a Line Plot

A line plot is a simple way to organize small amounts of data along a number line. After you draw the number line and write what numbers you will use, plot X's above each number to show each piece of data.

Length of Objects	Number of Objects
4 inches	3
5 inches	2
6 inches	5

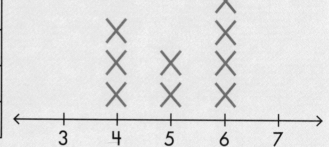

Choose 5 different writing tools (pen, pencil, crayon, marker, highlighter, etc.). Measure each tool to the nearest inch (you can use the ones from the previous page). Make a line plot organizing the data from the measurements you collected.

Lesson 5.10 Making a Line Plot

Make a line plot based on the information below.

4 sneakers	18 cm, 18 cm, 20 cm, 20 cm
6 flip flops	14 cm, 14 cm, 15 cm, 15 cm, 17 cm, 17 cm
2 high heels	15 cm, 15 cm
4 boots	20 cm, 20 cm, 19 cm, 19 cm

$\longleftarrow\!\!\!-\!\!\!-\!\!\!-\!\!\!-\!\!\!-\!\!\!-\!\!\!-\!\!\!-\!\!\!-\!\!\!\longrightarrow$

Lesson 5.10 Making a Line Plot

Create a line plot using the length of each side of each shape.

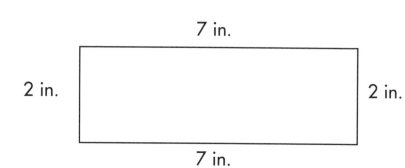

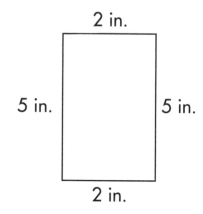

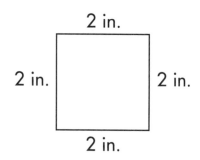

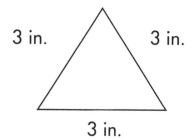

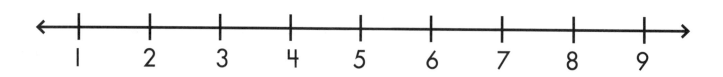

Lesson 5.10 Making a Line Plot

Create a line plot based on the measurements given below.

___7___ centimeters

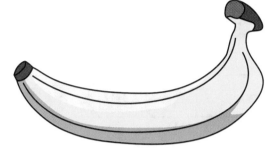

___10___ centimeters

___10___ centimeters

___10___ centimeters

___5___ centimeters

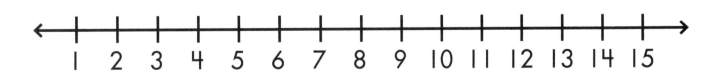

1 2 3 4 5 6 7 8 9 10 11 12 13 14 15

Lesson 5.11 Reading Picture Graphs

Ella asked her neighborhood friends about their pets. She made this picture graph to show the results. One animal picture means one pet.

OUR PETS

Dog	🐕 🐕 🐕 🐕 🐕 🐕
Cat	🐈 🐈 🐈 🐈 🐈 🐈 🐈 🐈
Fish	🐟 🐟 🐟 🐟 🐟
Turtle	🐢 🐢
None	I I I I

Use the picture graph to answer the questions.

How many pets do Ella's neighborhood friends have?

How many more fish and turtles are there than dogs?

Which animal is most popular?

NAME _____

Lesson 5.12 Creating Picture Graphs

Lamar looked around his house and counted the shapes of different objects. He wanted to create a picture graph to show his results.

Use the following clues to complete the picture graph.

- The fewest objects were shaped like a circle.
- 1 more object was shaped like a triangle than a circle.
- 2 fewer objects were shaped like a triangle than a square.
- 6 objects were shaped like a circle.
- 3 more objects were shaped like a star than a triangle.

Shapes Around the House

Triangles	
Stars	
Squares	
Circles	

Answer the questions based on the data from the picture graph.

How many objects are there in all?

How many more stars than triangles are there?

Spectrum Critical Thinking for Math
Grade 2

Lesson 5.12
Creating Picture Graphs
75

Lesson 5.13 Reading Bar Graphs

A total of 4 Walker Wildcats players scored in the basketball game last week. The points each player scored are shown in the bar graph.

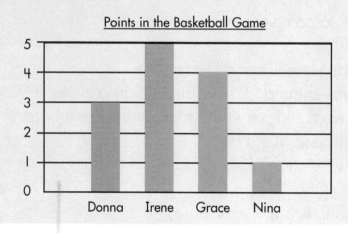

Points in the Basketball Game

Use the bar graph to answer the questions.

How many more points did Irene score than Nina?

How many total points did the Walker Wildcats score in last week's game?

How many points were scored by the 2 top scorers?

Lesson 5.14 Creating Bar Graphs

The members of a book club voted for their favorite fruits. They wanted to create a bar graph to show the results.

Use the following clues to complete the bar graph.

- The same amount of people chose apples, bananas, and pears.
- Grapes had the least number of votes.
- Apples had 2 fewer votes than oranges.
- Oranges got 6 votes.
- Grapes had more than 2 votes.

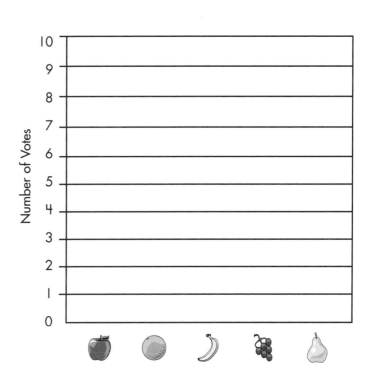

Answer the questions based on the data from the bar graph.

How many people are in the book club?

How many people voted for grapes and apples?

Check What You Learned

Measurement

1. Estimate the length of the paper clip. Then, use a ruler to measure the paper clip in inches and centimeters.

   Estimate: _____ in. _____ cm

   Actual: _____ in. _____ cm

2. Create a line plot based on the following data.
   12 cm, 12 cm, 15 cm, 14 cm, 13 cm, 14 cm, 14 cm, 15 cm, 16 cm, 12 cm, 13 cm

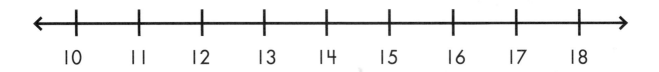

3. Owen sat down to eat dinner at 6:15 P.M. It took him 35 minutes to eat dinner. What time did Owen finish eating dinner? Show the time on both clocks below.

Check What You Learned

Measurement

Favorite Sports

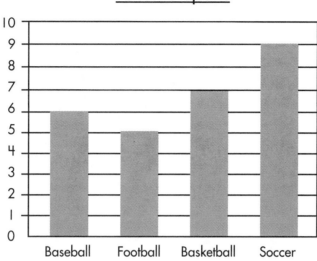

4. Use the information in the above bar graph to create a picture graph below.

Favorite Sports	
Baseball	
Football	
Basketball	
Soccer	

Use the graphs to answer the questions.

5. How many people were surveyed?

6. How many more people liked soccer and basketball than baseball and football?

Check What You Know

Geometry

Solve each riddle by drawing the shape it describes.

1. • I am a flat shape.
   • I have 3 sides.
   • I have 3 corners.
   What am I?

2. • I have 4 right angles.
   • I have 2 short sides and 2 long sides.
   • I am a flat shape.
   What am I?

3. • I have no sides.
   • I have no corners.
   • I am round and flat.
   What am I?

4. • I have 5 sides.
   • I have 5 angles.
   • I am flat.
   What am I?

Check What You Know

Geometry

5. At her birthday party, Tara received several gifts. One gift was in a box that had faces shaped like squares. The box had 6 faces and was wrapped in pretty green paper. What shape is the box? Draw the shape below.

6. James ordered some clothes from an online store. When his clothes were delivered, they were in a box. The box had 6 faces. 4 faces were shaped like rectangles, and 2 faces were shaped like squares. What shape is the box that James' clothes came in? Draw the shape below.

Lesson 6.1 Attributes of Plane Shapes

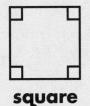 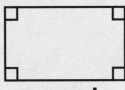 

square
- 4 equal sides
- 4 right angles

rectangle
- 2 pairs of equal sides
- 4 right angles

triangle
- 3 sides
- 3 angles

Is this shape a triangle? Explain why or why not.

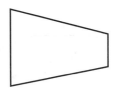

_____

_____

Is this shape a rectangle? Explain why or why not.

_____

_____

Lesson 6.1 Attributes of Plane Shapes

circle
- no sides
- no angles

pentagon
- 5 sides
- 5 angles

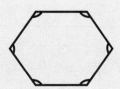

hexagon
- 6 sides
- 6 angles

Is this shape a pentagon? Explain why or why not.

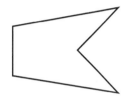

_____

_____

Is this shape a hexagon? Explain why or why not.

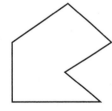

_____

_____

Lesson 6.2   Attributes of Solid Shapes

cube
• 6 square faces

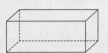

rectangular prism
• 6 rectangular faces

Is this an example of a cube? Explain why or why not.

_____

_____

Is this an example of a rectangular solid? Explain why or why not.

_____

_____

Lesson 6.2   Attributes of Solid Shapes

square pyramid
- 4 triangular faces
- 1 square face

sphere
- no faces
- perfectly round

Lucy says this beach ball is an example of a sphere. Is she correct? Explain why or why not.

_____

_____

Tony tells his friends that his soup can is the shape of a square pyramid. Is Tony correct? Explain why or why not.

_____

Lesson 6.3 Drawing Plane Shapes in the Real World

The following are examples of rectangles that you can find in the real world.

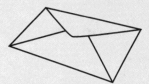

Draw 2 examples of each shape that you can find in the real world.

Lesson 6.4 Drawing Plane Shapes

This pattern is an A-B-C pattern:

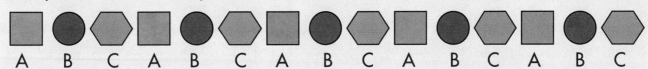

A B C A B C A B C A B C A B C

This pattern is an A-A-B pattern:

A A B A A B A A B A A B A A B

Create two different patterns using plane shapes only. Repeat and draw each pattern 3 times. Label your patterns.

Lesson 6.5 Drawing Solid Shapes in the Real World

The following are examples of a cylinder that you can find in the real world.

Draw 2 examples of each shape that you can find in the real world.

Lesson 6.6 Drawing Solid Shapes

This pattern is an A-B-C-C pattern:

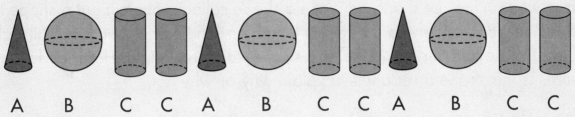

A   B   C   C   A   B   C   C   A   B   C   C

Create two different patterns using solid shapes only. Repeat and draw each pattern 3 times. Label your patterns.

Check What You Learned

Geometry

1. Denise was cutting out shapes to make a shape collage. She cut out a shape that had 4 sides. Each side was a different length and the corners were not all right angles. Denise told her friend that this shape was a rectangle. Her friend was unsure. Is this shape a rectangle? Explain why or why not.

2. The Lopez family is moving across the country. They are packing up everything in large and small boxes. Amy Lopez starts packing a box with 6 square faces. Fernando Lopez starts packing a box with 6 rectangular faces. Mr. Lopez says they are packing two different boxes, but Amy and Fernando say they are the same. Are the boxes the same? Explain why or why not.

Check What You Learned

Geometry

3. Brady did a shape walk around his house. He counted how many of each shape he saw in his house. Then, he organized the information in a tally chart. Use the tally chart to create a picture graph of shapes.

Shape	Number of Shapes
square pyramid	I I
cube	IIII I
triangle	I I I I
pentagon	I I I
hexagon	I I I

CHAPTER 6 POSTTEST

Shapes in Brady's House

square pyramid	
cube	
triangle	
pentagon	
hexagon	

NAME _____

Check What You Know

Parts of a Whole

1. Show 2 different ways to partition a rectangle in half.

2. Quinn divides his rectangular suitcase into 4 sections so he can pack shorts, shirts, pants, and pajamas for his trip. Show 2 different ways Quinn can divide his suitcase. Shade the section where he should pack pajamas in both drawings.

3. Vanessa bought a giant chocolate chip cookie for her mother's birthday. She cut the cookie into thirds and gave her mom $\frac{1}{3}$. Show 2 different ways Vanessa could have divided the cookie. Shade the piece she gave to her mom in both drawings.

Lesson 7.1 Partitioning Rectangles in the Real World

Chelsea ordered a rectangular pizza. She cut the pizza into fourths and ate $\frac{1}{4}$ of the pizza for lunch:

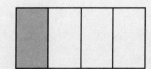

Here is another way Chelsea could have cut the pizza and eaten $\frac{1}{4}$ of the pizza:

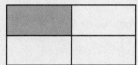

Jasper has a garden shaped like a rectangle. He divides his garden into fourths so he can plant corn, potatoes, carrots, and squash. Show 2 ways Jasper could divide up his garden. Then, shade where he should plant the squash.

Kevin and Kyle share a rectangular bedroom. They want to divide the room in half so they each have a side. Show 2 ways Kevin and Kyle can divide their bedroom. Then, shade Kyle's side of the room for each picture.

Lesson 7.2 Partitioning Circles in the Real World

Myra baked a circular apple pie. She cut the pie into thirds and ate $\frac{1}{3}$ of the pie:

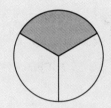

Here is another way Myra could have cut the pie and eaten $\frac{1}{3}$ of it:

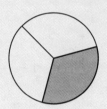

Luke made a circle-shaped cheese pizza for lunch. He divided the pizza into thirds and gave $\frac{1}{3}$ to his little brother. Show 2 ways Luke could divide the cheese pizza. Then, shade the part that Luke's little brother ate in both drawings.

Shannon has a circle-shaped swimming pool. She wants to divide the pool in half and put up a net so she can play pool volleyball with her family. Show 2 ways Shannon can divide the pool in half. Then, shade the side that Shannon will play on in both drawings.

Lesson 7.3   Partitioning Rectangles

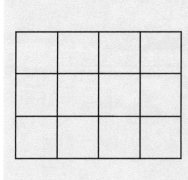 This rectangle
is divided into
3 rows and
4 columns. It
has 12 equal
squares.

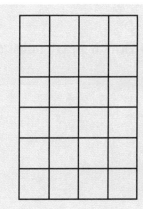 This rectangle
is divided into
6 rows and
4 columns. It
has 24 equal
squares.

Show four ways to divide the given rectangles into equal squares.

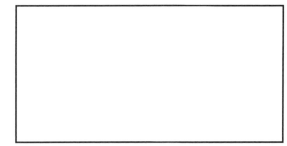

Check What You Learned

Parts of a Whole

1. Show 2 ways to partition a rectangle into equal squares.

2. Wallace invited some friends over to play games. He needed to divide his backyard in half for the dry games and the water games. Wallace's backyard is shaped like a rectangle. Show 2 ways Wallace could divide it. Shade the section where he should have the water games in both drawings.

3. Mrs. Robinson had 1 pie. She cut it into 4 equal pieces and ate 1 piece. Show 2 ways that Mrs. Robinson could divide up the pie. Shade the piece that she ate in both drawings.

Final Test Chapters 1-7

1. Draw an array to show the equation. Then, solve the equation. Circle whether the total is **even** or **odd**.

   3 + 3 + 3 + 3 + 3 =

   Total: _____

   Even or Odd

Solve the problem. Draw blocks to show your thinking.

2. Byron sold 343 raffle tickets at the basketball game. Alexa sold 438 tickets at the volleyball game. Dominique sold 800 raffle tickets at the talent show. How many total tickets did Byron and Alexa sell? How many more tickets did Dominique sell than Byron and Alexa combined?

Spectrum Critical Thinking for Math
Grade 2

Final Test Chapters 1-7

Solve. Use a number line to show your thinking.

Fiona is making a flower arrangement for her grandmother. She uses 5 white daisies, 5 pink daisies, 6 red roses, and 6 yellow roses.

3. How many daisies does Fiona use?

4. How many roses does Fiona use?

5. How many total flowers does Fiona use?

6. Write the equation that is detailed on the number line.

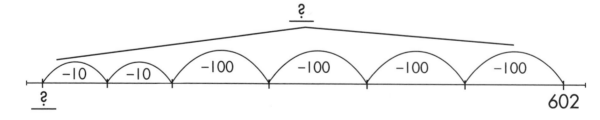

Final Test Chapters 1-7

Work with the number **378** in the following ways:

7. Write using number name.

8. Write using expanded form.

9. Compare 378 to 482 using blocks.

10. Nicole had a box of crackers. There were 741 crackers in the box. Nicole ate 105 crackers and shared 615 crackers with some friends. Did Nicole have any crackers left? If so, how many? Use a number line to show your thinking.

Final Test Chapters 1-7

11. Estimate the length of each object. Then, use a ruler to measure each object to the nearest inch and nearest centimeter.

Estimate: _____ in. _____ cm   Estimate: _____ in. _____ cm

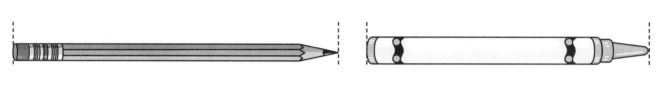

Actual: _____ in. _____ cm   Actual: _____ in. _____ cm

12. Create a line plot based on the following data.

4 in., 5 in., 6 in., 6 in., 5 in., 4 in., 9 in., 4 in., 5 in., 4 in., 6 in.

Spectrum Critical Thinking for Math
Grade 2
100

Chapters 1-7
Final Test

CHAPTERS 1-7 FINAL TEST

Final Test Chapters 1-7

Madeline counted how many of each shape she saw on the playground and organized the information in a bar graph.

13. Use the bar graph to create a picture graph of the shapes.

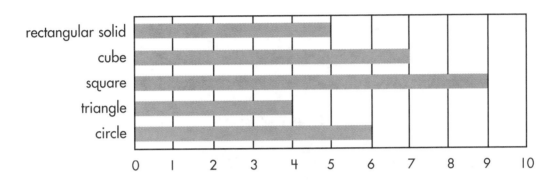

Shapes on the Playground

rectangular solid	
cube	
square	
triangle	
circle	

14. How many total shapes did Madeline count on the playground?

15. How many more objects would she need to count to get to 50 shapes?

Spectrum Critical Thinking for Math
Grade 2

Chapters 1-7
Final Test

CHAPTERS 1-7 FINAL TEST

101

Final Test Chapters 1-7

Olivia is sorting shapes. She finds 2 shapes, but she can't remember their names. Help Olivia name each shape by reading the description she gives.

16. This shape is a solid shape. It has 6 square faces and a lot of corners.

_____

17. This shape has 4 sides and 4 corners. It has 2 long sides and 2 short sides and all of the corners are right angles.

_____

18. Trent's mom bakes a batch of brownies in a rectangular pan for Trent to bring to his chess club meeting. Trent is not sure how many people will come to this meeting. Last month, only 4 members showed up. But the month before that, all 12 members came. Show how Trent can divide the brownies into fourths if 4 members attend. Then, show how Trent can partition the brownies equally if all 12 members attend.

CHAPTERS 1-7 FINAL TEST

Spectrum Critical Thinking for Math
Grade 2
102

Chapters 1-7
Final Test

Answer Key

Page 5

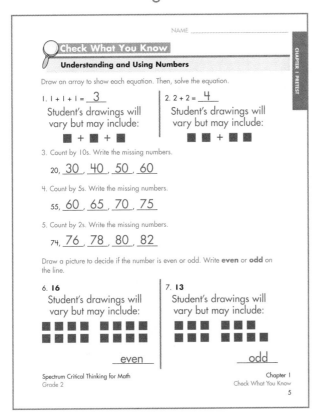

Check What You Know

Understanding and Using Numbers

CHAPTER 1 PRETEST

Draw an array to show each equation. Then, solve the equation.

1. 1 + 1 + 1 = __3__
Student's drawings will vary but may include:
■ + ■ + ■

2. 2 + 2 = __4__
Student's drawings will vary but may include:
■■ + ■■

3. Count by 10s. Write the missing numbers.
20, __30__, __40__, __50__, __60__

4. Count by 5s. Write the missing numbers.
55, __60__, __65__, __70__, __75__

5. Count by 2s. Write the missing numbers.
74, __76__, __78__, __80__, __82__

Draw a picture to decide if the number is even or odd. Write **even** or **odd** on the line.

6. **16**
Student's drawings will vary but may include:
__even__

7. **13**
Student's drawings will vary but may include:
__odd__

Spectrum Critical Thinking for Math
Grade 2

Chapter 1
Check What You Know
5

Page 6

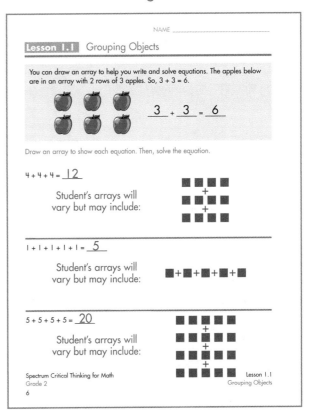

Lesson 1.1 Grouping Objects

You can draw an array to help you write and solve equations. The apples below are in an array with 2 rows of 3 apples. So, 3 + 3 = 6.

__3__ + __3__ = __6__

Draw an array to show each equation. Then, solve the equation.

4 + 4 + 4 = __12__
Student's arrays will vary but may include:

1 + 1 + 1 + 1 + 1 = __5__
Student's arrays will vary but may include:
■+■+■+■+■

5 + 5 + 5 + 5 = __20__
Student's arrays will vary but may include:

Spectrum Critical Thinking for Math
Grade 2

Lesson 1.1
Grouping Objects
6

Page 7

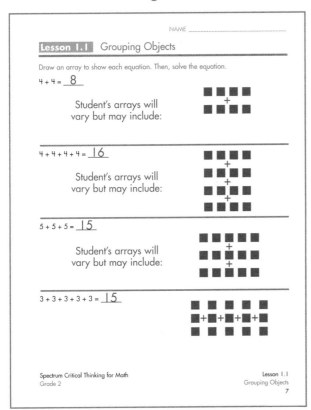

Lesson 1.1 Grouping Objects

Draw an array to show each equation. Then, solve the equation.

4 + 4 = __8__
Student's arrays will vary but may include:

4 + 4 + 4 + 4 = __16__
Student's arrays will vary but may include:

5 + 5 + 5 = __15__
Student's arrays will vary but may include:

3 + 3 + 3 + 3 + 3 = __15__

Spectrum Critical Thinking for Math
Grade 2

Lesson 1.1
Grouping Objects
7

Page 8

Lesson 1.2 Skip Counting

To skip count, take the amount you are skip counting by and add on to the previous number.

+2 +2 +2 +2
2 4 6 8 10

+5 +5 +5 +5
5 10 15 20 25

+10 +10 +10 +10
10 20 30 40 50

Count by 2. Write the missing numbers.
20, __22__, __24__, __26__, 28, __30__, __32__, __34__, 36

Count by 5. Write the missing numbers.
35, __40__, __45__, __50__, 55, __60__, __65__, __70__, 75

Count by 10. Write the missing numbers.
__30__, __40__, __50__, 60, __70__, __80__, __90__, 100

Spectrum Critical Thinking for Math
Grade 2

Lesson 1.2
Skip Counting
8

Answer Key

Page 9

NAME

Lesson 1.2 Skip Counting

Start at 12. Count by 2s. Write as many numbers as you can.

Accept all consecutive numbers divisible by 2 and starting with 12.

Start at 45. Count by 5s. Write as many numbers as you can.

Accept all consecutive numbers divisible by 5 and starting with 45.

Start at 20. Count by 10s. Write as many numbers as you can.

Accept all consecutive numbers divisible by 10 and starting with 20

Page 10

NAME

Lesson 1.3 Even or Odd?

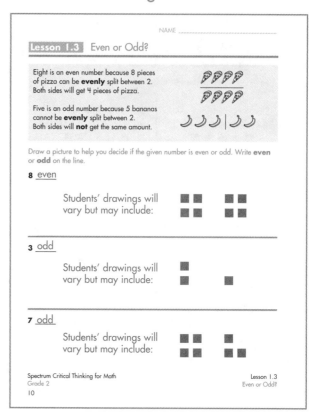

Eight is an even number because 8 pieces of pizza can be **evenly** split between 2. Both sides will get 4 pieces of pizza.

Five is an odd number because 5 bananas cannot be **evenly** split between 2. Both sides will **not** get the same amount.

Draw a picture to help you decide if the given number is even or odd. Write **even** or **odd** on the line.

8 even

Students' drawings will vary but may include:

3 odd

Students' drawings will vary but may include:

7 odd

Students' drawings will vary but may include:

Spectrum Critical Thinking for Math
Grade 2
10

Lesson 1.3
Even or Odd?

Page 11

NAME

Lesson 1.3 Even or Odd?

Draw a picture to help you decide if the given number is even or odd. Write **even** or **odd** on the line.

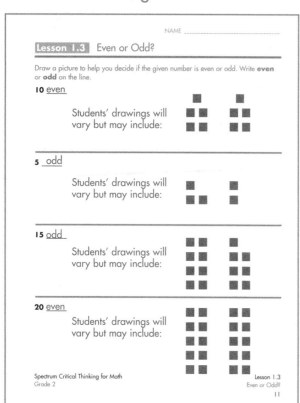

10 even

Students' drawings will vary but may include:

5 odd

Students' drawings will vary but may include:

15 odd

Students' drawings will vary but may include:

20 even

Students' drawings will vary but may include:

Spectrum Critical Thinking for Math
Grade 2

Lesson 1.3
Even or Odd?
11

Page 12

NAME

💡 **Check What You Learned**

Understanding and Using Numbers

Draw an array to show each equation. Then, solve the equation. Decide if each total is even or odd. Circle **even** or **odd**.

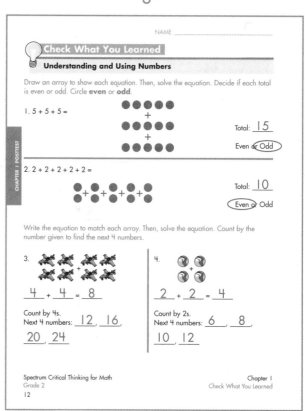

1. $5 + 5 + 5 =$ Total: 15   Even or (Odd)

2. $2 + 2 + 2 + 2 + 2 =$ Total: 10   (Even) or Odd

Write the equation to match each array. Then, solve the equation. Count by the number given to find the next 4 numbers.

3. $\underline{4} + \underline{4} = \underline{8}$

Count by 4s.
Next 4 numbers: 12, 16, 20, 24

4. $\underline{2} + \underline{2} = \underline{4}$

Count by 2s.
Next 4 numbers: 6, 8, 10, 12

CHAPTER 1 POSTTEST

Spectrum Critical Thinking for Math
Grade 2
12

Chapter 1
Check What You Learned

Answer Key

Page 13

Check What You Know

CHAPTER 2 PRETEST

Addition and Subtraction Through 20

Add or subtract. Draw models to show your thinking.

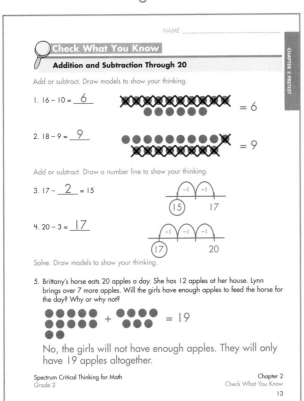

1. $16 - 10 = \underline{6}$ = 6

2. $18 - 9 = \underline{9}$ = 9

Add or subtract. Draw a number line to show your thinking.

3. $17 - \underline{2} = 15$

4. $20 - 3 = \underline{17}$

Solve. Draw models to show your thinking.

5. Brittany's horse eats 20 apples a day. She has 12 apples at her house. Lynn brings over 7 more apples. Will the girls have enough apples to feed the horse for the day? Why or why not?

$\bullet\bullet\bullet\bullet + \bullet\bullet\bullet = 19$

No, the girls will not have enough apples. They will only have 19 apples altogether.

Spectrum Critical Thinking for Math
Grade 2

Chapter 2
Check What You Know
13

Page 14

Lesson 2.1 Drawing a Picture to Add

You can draw a picture to help you solve an addition problem.

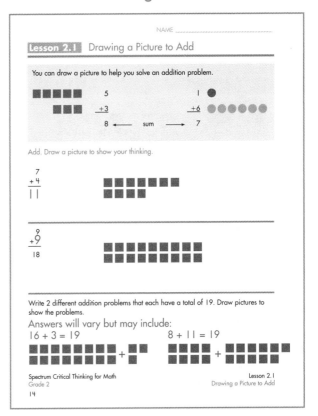

$\begin{array}{r} 5 \\ +3 \\ \hline 8 \end{array}$ ← sum → $\begin{array}{r} 1 \\ +6 \\ \hline 7 \end{array}$

Add. Draw a picture to show your thinking.

$\begin{array}{r} 7 \\ +4 \\ \hline 11 \end{array}$

$\begin{array}{r} 9 \\ +9 \\ \hline 18 \end{array}$

Write 2 different addition problems that each have a total of 19. Draw pictures to show the problems.

Answers will vary but may include:

$16 + 3 = 19$ $8 + 11 = 19$

Spectrum Critical Thinking for Math
Grade 2
14

Lesson 2.1
Drawing a Picture to Add

Page 15

Lesson 2.2 Drawing a Picture to Subtract

You can draw a picture to help you solve a subtraction problem.

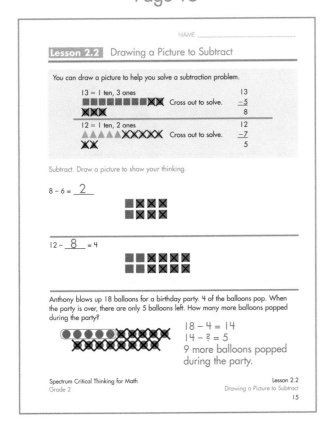

13 = 1 ten, 3 ones   Cross out to solve. $\begin{array}{r} 13 \\ -5 \\ \hline 8 \end{array}$

12 = 1 ten, 2 ones   Cross out to solve. $\begin{array}{r} 12 \\ -7 \\ \hline 5 \end{array}$

Subtract. Draw a picture to show your thinking.

$8 - 6 = \underline{2}$

$12 - \underline{8} = 4$

Anthony blows up 18 balloons for a birthday party. 4 of the balloons pop. When the party is over, there are only 5 balloons left. How many more balloons popped during the party?

$18 - 4 = 14$
$14 - ? = 5$
9 more balloons popped during the party.

Spectrum Critical Thinking for Math
Grade 2

Lesson 2.2
Drawing a Picture to Subtract
15

Page 16

Lesson 2.3 Using a Number Line to Add

You can use a number line to add. Start at one addend, and count on the number line using the other addend. The number you stop on is your answer.

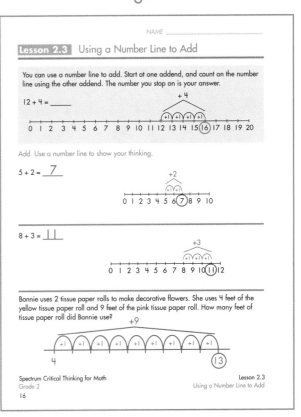

$12 + 4 = \underline{}$

Add. Use a number line to show your thinking.

$5 + 2 = \underline{7}$

$8 + 3 = \underline{11}$

Bonnie uses 2 tissue paper rolls to make decorative flowers. She uses 4 feet of the yellow tissue paper roll and 9 feet of the pink tissue paper roll. How many feet of tissue paper roll did Bonnie use?

Spectrum Critical Thinking for Math
Grade 2
16

Lesson 2.3
Using a Number Line to Add

Answer Key

Page 17

NAME _____

Lesson 2.4 Using a Number Line to Subtract

You can use a number line to solve subtraction problems. Start at the number you are subtracting from. Count down by the amount you are subtracting. The number you stop on is your answer.

$17 - 7 =$ _____

Subtract. Use a number line to show your thinking.

$20 - 5 = \underline{15}$

$14 - 6 = \underline{8}$

Deanna has 16 crayons. She gives 5 crayons to her little sister. How many crayons does Deanna have left?

Deanna has
11 crayons left.

Page 18

NAME _____

Lesson 2.5 Solving Problems by Adding On

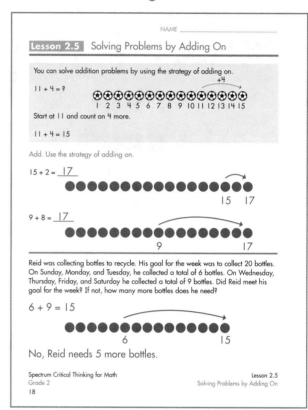

You can solve addition problems by using the strategy of adding on.

$11 + 4 = ?$

Start at 11 and count on 4 more.

$11 + 4 = 15$

Add. Use the strategy of adding on.

$15 + 2 = \underline{17}$

$9 + 8 = \underline{17}$

Reid was collecting bottles to recycle. His goal for the week was to collect 20 bottles. On Sunday, Monday, and Tuesday, he collected a total of 6 bottles. On Wednesday, Thursday, Friday, and Saturday he collected a total of 9 bottles. Did Reid meet his goal for the week? If not, how many more bottles does he need?

$6 + 9 = 15$

No, Reid needs 5 more bottles.

Page 19

NAME _____

Lesson 2.6 Using Addition for Subtraction

You can use addition to solve subtraction problems.

$15 - 6 = ?$ Think: $6 + ? = 15$.

Use strategies such as counting on, drawing a picture, or using a number line to solve the addition problem.

$6 + 9 = 15$, so $15 - 6 = 9$

Solve. Use addition to help you show your thinking.

Mr. Chadwick has 18 fish in his aquarium. 8 of the fish are catfish. The others are zebrafish. Explain how you can figure out how many of the fish are zebrafish by using addition.

$8 + ? = 18$ You can add on to 8 until you reach 18.
$8 + 10 = 18$ You would need to add 10 more.

Next week, Mr. Chadwick will have 25 living things in his aquarium after he adds plants and snails. Write a subtraction sentence to show how many plants and snails Mr. Chadwick will add to the aquarium.

$25 - 18 = 7$
Mr. Chadwick is going to add 7 plants and snails to his aquarium.

Page 20

NAME _____

Lesson 2.7 Addition and Subtraction

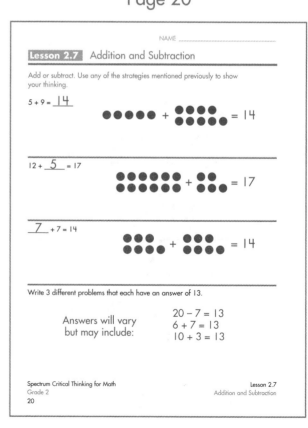

Add or subtract. Use any of the strategies mentioned previously to show your thinking.

$5 + 9 = \underline{14}$

$12 + \underline{5} = 17$

$\underline{7} + 7 = 14$

Write 3 different problems that each have an answer of 13.

Answers will vary
but may include:

$20 - 7 = 13$
$6 + 7 = 13$
$10 + 3 = 13$

Answer Key

Page 21

NAME

Lesson 2.8 Adding and Subtracting in the Real World

Erika caught 8 fish at the pond. April caught 12 more fish. They decided to put 5 fish back. How many fish did Erika and April take home?

First, find how many fish they caught altogether.

8 + 12 = ?

Next, solve to find how many fish Erika and April got to take home.

20 − 5 = ?

Erika and April got to take home 15 fish.

Solve the problem. Draw pictures to show your thinking.

Ivy made 10 cupcakes for the bake sale. Hannah made 10 chocolate-covered pretzels. On the way to the sale, 2 pretzels broke and 1 cupcake fell on the ground. How many baked goods do the girls have to sell now?

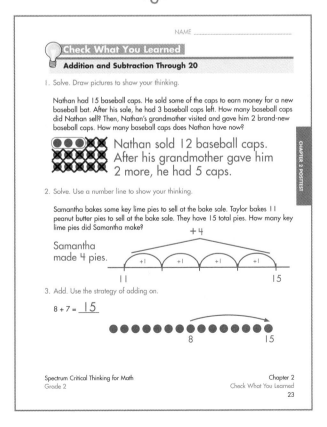

= 17   The girls have 17 baked goods to sell.

Page 22

NAME

Lesson 2.8 Adding and Subtracting in the Real World

Solve the problems. Show your work.

The toy store has 18 toy cars left in stock. On Monday, it sells 8 of the cars. On Tuesday, it sells 3 more of the cars. On Wednesday, Mark comes to the store and wants to buy a toy car. Are there any left for Mark to buy? Use a number line to show your thinking.

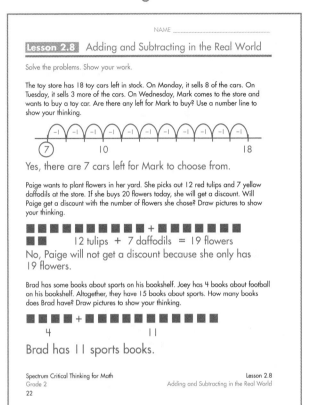

Yes, there are 7 cars left for Mark to choose from.

Paige wants to plant flowers in her yard. She picks out 12 red tulips and 7 yellow daffodils at the store. If she buys 20 flowers today, she will get a discount. Will Paige get a discount with the number of flowers she chose? Draw pictures to show your thinking.

12 tulips + 7 daffodils = 19 flowers

No, Paige will not get a discount because she only has 19 flowers.

Brad has some books about sports on his bookshelf. Joey has 4 books about football on his bookshelf. Altogether, they have 15 books about sports. How many books does Brad have? Draw pictures to show your thinking.

4 + 11

Brad has 11 sports books.

Page 23

NAME

💡 **Check What You Learned**

Addition and Subtraction Through 20

1. Solve. Draw pictures to show your thinking.

Nathan had 15 baseball caps. He sold some of the caps to earn money for a new baseball bat. After his sale, he had 3 baseball caps left. How many baseball caps did Nathan sell? Then, Nathan's grandmother visited and gave him 2 brand-new baseball caps. How many baseball caps does Nathan have now?

Nathan sold 12 baseball caps. After his grandmother gave him 2 more, he had 5 caps.

2. Solve. Use a number line to show your thinking.

Samantha bakes some key lime pies to sell at the bake sale. Taylor bakes 11 peanut butter pies to sell at the bake sale. They have 15 total pies. How many key lime pies did Samantha make?

Samantha made 4 pies.

+4
+1 +1 +1 +1
11   15

3. Add. Use the strategy of adding on.

8 + 7 = 15

8   15

CHAPTER 2 POSTTEST

Page 24

NAME

🔍 **Check What You Know**

Addition and Subtraction with 2-Digit Numbers

Solve. Draw pictures to show your thinking.

1. 12 + 27 = 39

+ = 39

2. 49 − 48 = 1

= 1

Solve. Use a number line to show your thinking.

3. 10 + 30 = ____

+10 +10 +10
10   40

4. 84 − 71 = ____

−1 −10 −10 −10 −10 −10 −10 −10
13 14   84

Solve the problem. Draw pictures to show your thinking.

5. Westberg's Pizza Shop sells pizza by the slice. On Monday, it sold 37 slices. On Tuesday, it sold 50 slices. The goal for the week was 99 slices. Do you think the shop will meet its goal? Why or why not?

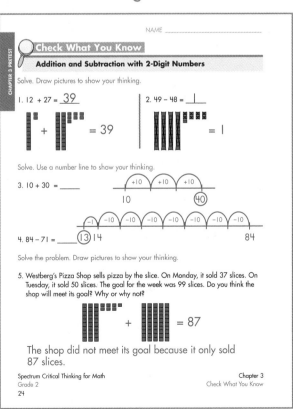

+ = 87

The shop did not meet its goal because it only sold 87 slices.

CHAPTER 3 PRETEST

Answer Key

Page 25

NAME

Lesson 3.1 Adding with Tens and Ones Blocks

You can use tens and ones blocks to help you solve a problem.

$\begin{array}{r} 25 \\ + 43 \\ \hline \end{array}$

Add the ones. 8 ones
Add the tens. 6 tens
25 + 43 = 68

Add. Draw tens and ones blocks to show your thinking.

$\begin{array}{r} 36 \\ + 43 \\ \hline \end{array}$

$\begin{array}{r} + \\ \hline 79 \end{array}$

Write the problem for the tens and ones blocks shown.

$\underline{27} + \underline{31} = \underline{58}$

Draw another way to show this problem with tens and ones blocks.

Answers will vary but may include:

 = 58

Spectrum Critical Thinking for Math
Grade 2

Lesson 3.1
Adding with Tens and Ones Blocks
25

Page 26

NAME

Lesson 3.2 Subtracting with Tens and Ones Blocks

You can draw tens and ones blocks to help you subtract.

$\begin{array}{r} 77 \\ - 26 \\ \hline \end{array}$

There are 5 tens and 1 one left.
So, the answer is 51.

Subtract. Draw tens and ones blocks to show your thinking.

$\begin{array}{r} 49 \\ - 39 \\ \hline \end{array}$

 = 10

Using tens and ones blocks, write a subtraction problem with an answer of 21. Write a word problem to go with the subtraction problem.

$39 - 18 = 21$

Word problems will vary.

Spectrum Critical Thinking for Math
Grade 2
26

Lesson 3.2
Subtracting with Tens and Ones Blocks

Page 27

NAME

Lesson 3.3 Using a Number Line to Add

You can add 2-digit numbers using a number line. Break the second addend into tens and ones.

40 + 34 = ?

40 + 34 = 74

Add. Use a number line to show your thinking.

$\begin{array}{r} 66 \\ + 22 \\ \hline \end{array}$

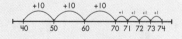

66   76   86   (88)

Charlotte had 34 bean plants. Mika had 53 bean plants. Then, Charlotte and Mika were given 13 more plants by a neighbor. How many plants do they have now?

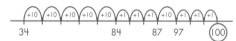

34   84   87   97   (100)

Charlotte and Mika now have 100 plants.

Spectrum Critical Thinking for Math
Grade 2

Lesson 3.3
Using a Number Line to Add
27

Page 28

NAME

Lesson 3.4 Using a Number Line to Subtract

You can subtract 2-digit numbers using a number line.

82 − 51 = ?

31 32   42   52   62   72   82

82 − 51 = 31

Subtract. Use a number line to show your thinking.

36 − 24 = 12

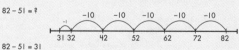

(12)   36

Write the subtraction problem for the number line given.

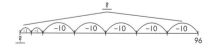

$\underline{96} - \underline{52} = \underline{44}$

Spectrum Critical Thinking for Math
Grade 2
28

Lesson 3.4
Using a Number Line to Subtract

Answer Key

Page 29

NAME _____

Lesson 3.5 Finding Missing Numbers

You can use different strategies to find a missing addend in an addition problem:
42 + _____ = 97.
Begin with the largest number in the problem. Subtract the smaller number to find the missing value.

Draw a picture.   **Use a number line.**

42 + 55 = 97

Solve. Draw a picture or number line to show your thinking.

Upton went to the grocery store. He bought a banana for 35 cents. He also bought a melon. He spent 83 cents total. How much did Upton spend on the melon?

35 + ? = 83
Upton spent 48 cents on the melon.   = 48

Brooke went to the grocery store and bought an apple for 20 cents. She also bought an orange. She spent 53 cents total. How much did Brooke spend on the orange?

Brooke spent 33 cents on the orange.

− 20
33   53

Spectrum Critical Thinking for Math
Grade 2

Lesson 3.5
Finding Missing Numbers
29

Page 30

NAME _____

Lesson 3.5 Finding Missing Numbers

You can use different strategies to find a missing number in a subtraction problem: 69 − _____ = 44.
Begin with the largest number in the problem. Subtract the smaller number to find the missing value.

Draw a picture.   **Use a number line.**

69 − 25 = 44

Subtract. Draw a picture or number line to show your thinking.

Connor buys a crayon and a pen for 99 cents. The pen costs 65 cents. How much does the crayon cost?

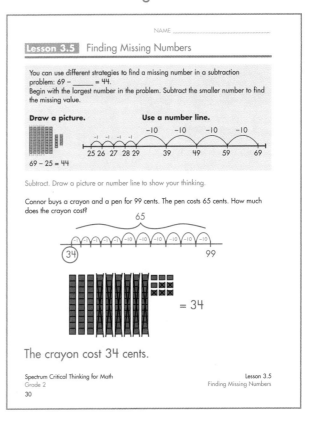

The crayon cost 34 cents.

Spectrum Critical Thinking for Math
Grade 2
30

Lesson 3.5
Finding Missing Numbers

Page 31

NAME _____

Lesson 3.6 Adding and Subtracting in the Real World

You can solve word problems using strategies such as drawing a picture, using a number line, or writing an equation.

There were 28 dogs in the dog park on Saturday. Some dogs left the park. There are 14 dogs remaining. How many dogs left?

Write an equation.   **Use a number line.**   **Draw a picture.**
28 − ? = 14   28 − 14 = 14
14 dogs left the dog park.

Solve the problem with a number line and with blocks.

Derek finds 23 frogs at the pond, but 12 hop away. Justin finds 29 frogs at the lake, but 21 hop away. How many frogs do Derek and Justin have?

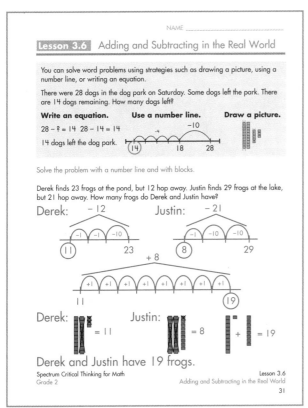

Derek and Justin have 19 frogs.

Spectrum Critical Thinking for Math
Grade 2

Lesson 3.6
Adding and Subtracting in the Real World
31

Page 32

NAME _____

Lesson 3.6 Adding and Subtracting in the Real World

Solve the problems. Show your answer using both a number line and tens and ones blocks.

Murphy Elementary School had 88 cartons of milk on Monday. After breakfast, there were 25 cartons left in the cooler. How many cartons of milk did the school serve for breakfast?

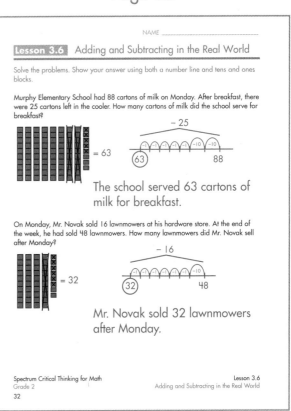

The school served 63 cartons of milk for breakfast.

On Monday, Mr. Novak sold 16 lawnmowers at his hardware store. At the end of the week, he had sold 48 lawnmowers. How many lawnmowers did Mr. Novak sell after Monday?

Mr. Novak sold 32 lawnmowers after Monday.

Spectrum Critical Thinking for Math
Grade 2
32

Lesson 3.6
Adding and Subtracting in the Real World

Answer Key

Page 33

NAME _____

Lesson 3.7 Addition with Renaming

You can draw tens and ones blocks to help you add 2-digit numbers.

$$\begin{array}{r} 36 \\ + 45 \end{array}$$ 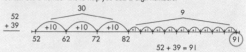 $= \boxed{81}$

Count the ones.
Trade in 10 ones for a tens block.
Count the tens and the ones left over.

Add. Draw tens and ones blocks to show your thinking.

Jimmy runs a lemonade stand at the end of his driveway for 4 weeks during the summer. The table shows how much he made each week.

Week 1	$24
Week 2	$29
Week 3	$28
Week 4	$27

How much money did Jimmy make altogether in Week 1 and Week 2?

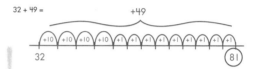 = 53

Spectrum Critical Thinking for Math
Grade 2

Lesson 3.7
Addition with Renaming
33

Page 34

NAME _____

Lesson 3.7 Addition with Renaming

You can use a number line to help you add 2-digit numbers.

$$\begin{array}{r} 52 \\ + 39 \end{array}$$

$52 + 39 = 91$

Start your number line at the first number given (52).
Using tens, count forward by the number of tens you are adding (30).
Using ones, count forward by the number of ones you are adding (9).
The number you land on is the answer.

Add. Use a number line to show your thinking.

$32 + 49 =$

Write the number sentence for the problem shown on the number line.

$\underline{29} + \underline{13} = \underline{42}$

Spectrum Critical Thinking for Math
Grade 2
34

Lesson 3.7
Addition with Renaming

Page 35

NAME _____

Lesson 3.8 Subtraction with Renaming

You can draw tens and ones blocks to help you subtract 2-digit numbers.

$$\begin{array}{r} 33 \\ - 18 \end{array}$$ $33 - 18 = 15$

Take away the ones. You will need to break up a tens block.
Go to the tens. Cross out the 1 ten you are subtracting.
Count the tens and ones blocks you have left.

Subtract. Draw tens and ones blocks to show your thinking.

62 birds are perching in the big oak tree. 29 birds fly away. How many birds are left in the tree?

 = 33

Another 14 birds fly away. How many are left in the tree now?

 = 19

Spectrum Critical Thinking for Math
Grade 2

Lesson 3.8
Subtraction with Renaming
35

Page 36

NAME _____

Lesson 3.8 Subtraction with Renaming

You can subtract 2-digit numbers using a number line.

$$\begin{array}{r} 52 \\ - 26 \end{array}$$

$52 - 26 = 26$

Start your number line with the first number given.
Using tens, count backward by the number of tens you are subtracting (20).
Using ones, count backward by the number of ones you are subtracting (6).
The number you land on is the answer (26).

Subtract. Use a number line to show your work.

Becky and Tina go on a nature walk. Becky finds 33 snails. Tina finds 28 snails. How many more snails does Becky find than Tina?

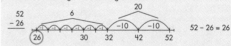

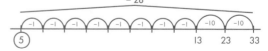

Becky found 5 more snails than Tina.

If 2 of Becky's snails slither away, how does that change your answer?

If 2 snails slithered away the answer would change to only 3 more snails than Tina.

Spectrum Critical Thinking for Math
Grade 2
36

Lesson 3.8
Subtraction with Renaming

Answer Key

Page 37

NAME _____

Lesson 3.9 Renaming in the Real World

Solve the problems.

Scott has 31 toy cars. He gives some of them to a friend. Now he has only 15 toy cars. How may toy cars did Scott give to his friend? Draw tens and ones blocks to show your thinking.

 → = 16

Rachel's class collects 38 cans of food for the food drive. Wesley's class collects 45 cans of food. The goal for the 2 classes is to collect 80 cans of food. Did the classes meet their goal? Draw a number line to show your thinking.

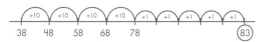

Yes, they met their goal because they collected 83 canned goods.

Page 38

NAME _____

Lesson 3.9 Renaming in the Real World

Write a word problem to go with the subtraction problem. Solve the problem by drawing a number line.

$65 - 39 =$ 26

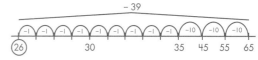

Word problems will vary.

_____

_____

_____

_____

_____

_____

_____

_____

Page 39

NAME _____

Check What You Learned

Addition and Subtraction with 2-Digit Numbers

1. Add or subtract. Draw models to show your thinking.

   Caitlyn has $87 in her piggy bank. She buys a new dress for $55. How much money does she have left? Use tens and ones blocks to show your thinking.

   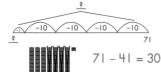 = 32
   Caitlyn has $32 left.

2. Add or subtract. Use a number line to show your thinking.

   Caitlyn wants to buy a new pair of sandals that costs $47. How much more money will she need? Use a number line to show your thinking.

   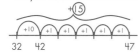 Caitlyn will need $15 more.

3. Write the number sentence that goes with the number line shown below. Then, show the problem using tens and ones blocks.

   $71 - 41 = 30$

Page 40

NAME _____

Mid-Test Chapters 1-3

Draw an array to show each equation. Then, solve the equation. Show if each total is even or odd by circling **even** or **odd**.

1. $3 + 3 + 3 + 3 =$ Total: 12 (Even) or Odd

2. $5 + 5 + 5 =$ Total: 15 Even or (Odd)

Write the equation to match each array. Then, solve the equation. Count by the amount given to find the next 4 numbers.

3. 7 + 7 + 7 = 21
   Count by 7s.
   Next 4 numbers: 28, 35, 42, 49

4. 6 + 6 + 6 + 6 = 24
   Count by 6s.
   Next 4 numbers: 30, 36, 42, 48

Answer Key

Page 41

Mid-Test Chapters 1-3

Solve the problems.

5. On Saturday, Michelle found 9 sand dollars at the beach. On Sunday, she found 4 more sand dollars. On her way home from the beach, 7 of the sand dollars broke. How many sand dollars does Michelle have left? Draw a picture to show your thinking.

● ● ● ● ● ● ✕ ✕ ✕ + ✕ ✕ ✕ ✕ = 6

Michelle has 6 sand dollars left.

6. Logan needs 15 rubber bands to finish making his rubber band ball. He finds 7 after school. How many more rubber bands does he need to finish? Draw a picture to show your thinking.

● ● ● ● ● ● ● ● ✕ ✕ ✕ ✕ ✕ ✕ ✕ = 8

Logan needs 8 more rubber bands.

7. Write the equation for the models shown below. Then, draw the problem on a number line.

 + ▯ 10 + 7 = 17

10 ⌒+1⌒+1⌒+1⌒+1⌒+1⌒+1⌒+1 (17)

CHAPTERS 1-3 MID-TEST

Page 42

Mid-Test Chapters 1-3

Solve the problems. Draw pictures to show your thinking.

8. At the county fair, children can play games and earn tickets for prizes. Shelby wants the large teddy bear that costs 100 tickets. She has 36 tickets. How many more tickets does she need?

Shelby needs 64 more tickets to get the teddy bear.

9. Shelby's brother gives her 25 of his tickets. Can she get the bear now?

 = 61   Shelby will have 61 tickets after her brother gives her 25. She still won't have enough for the bear.

Solve the problems. Use a number line to show your thinking.

10. William and Tyler each have 24 pennies. Denise has 31 pennies. How many pennies do William and Tyler have in all?

24 ⌒+10⌒+10⌒+1⌒+1⌒+1⌒+1 (48)

William and Tyler have 48 pennies.

11. How many pennies do all 3 children have in all?

⌒+10⌒+10⌒+10⌒+1
48   (79)

William, Tyler, and Denise have 79 pennies total.

CHAPTERS 1-3 MID-TEST

Page 43

🔍 **Check What You Know**

Working with 3-Digit Numbers

Complete problems 1–3 with the number **437**.

1. Show the number in expanded form.

400 + 30 + 7

2. Show the number in number name form.

Four hundred thirty-seven

3. Skip count backward by 2s to show the next 4 numbers.

435 , 433 , 431 , 429

4. Use a number line to compare:

847 ____>____ 625

625 ⌒+100⌒+100⌒+10⌒+10⌒+1⌒+1 (847)
      725   825   845

CHAPTER 4 PRETEST

Page 44

🔍 **Check What You Know**

Working with 3-Digit Numbers

5. Add. Use a number line to show your thinking.

641 + 208 = 849

641 ⌒+100⌒+100⌒+1⌒+1⌒+1⌒+1⌒+1⌒+1⌒+1⌒+1 (849)
       741   841

6. Subtract. Use blocks to show your thinking.

181 – 57 = 124

 →

7. Solve the problem. Use a number line to show your work.

Abigail collected 155 bottle caps to make jewelry. When she got home from school, she noticed that she only had 60 bottle caps in her kit. How many bottle caps did Abigail lose? She needs 100 bottle caps to make a necklace and a bracelet. How many more bottle caps does she need to be able to make the necklace and bracelet?

– 60
(95) ⌒–10⌒–10⌒–10⌒–10⌒–10⌒–10 155

+ 40
60 ⌒+10⌒+10⌒+10⌒+10 100

Abigail lost 95 bottle caps.   Abigail needs 40 more bottle caps.

CHAPTER 4 PRETEST

Answer Key

Page 45

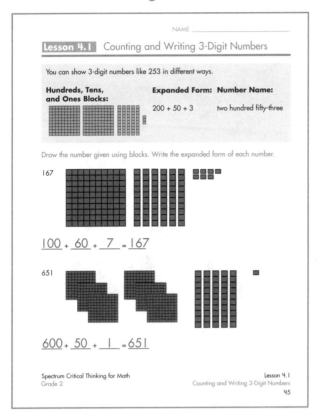

Lesson 4.1 Counting and Writing 3-Digit Numbers

You can show 3-digit numbers like 253 in different ways.

Hundreds, Tens, and Ones Blocks:

Expanded Form: 200 + 50 + 3

Number Name: two hundred fifty-three

Draw the number given using blocks. Write the expanded form of each number.

167

$\underline{100} + \underline{60} + \underline{7} = \underline{167}$

651

$\underline{600} + \underline{50} + \underline{1} = \underline{651}$

Page 46

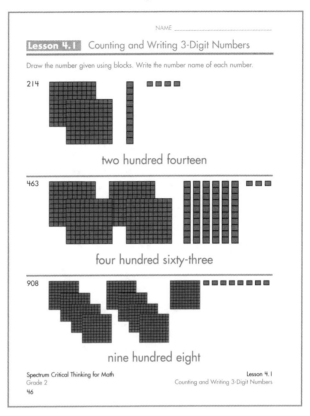

Lesson 4.1 Counting and Writing 3-Digit Numbers

Draw the number given using blocks. Write the number name of each number.

214

two hundred fourteen

463

four hundred sixty-three

908

nine hundred eight

Page 47

Lesson 4.2 Skip Counting with 3-Digit Numbers

Start at each number given. Skip count by the number given. Write as many numbers as you can.

1. Start at 200. Count by 10s.

200, 210, 220, 230, 240, 250, 260, 270, 280, 290, 300, 310, 320, 330, 340, 350, 360, 370, 380, 390, 400, 410, 420, 430

2. Start at 532. Count by 2s.

532, 534, 536, 538, 540, 542, 544, 546, 548, 550, 552, 554, 556, 558, 560, 562, 564, 566, 568, 570, 572, 574, 576, 578

3. Start at 300. Count backward by 5s.

300, 295, 290, 285, 280, 275, 270, 265, 260, 255, 250, 245, 240, 235, 230, 225, 220, 215, 210, 205, 200, 195, 190, 185

4. Start at 100. Count by 100s.

100, 200, 300, 400, 500, 600, 700, 800, 900, 1,000, 1,100, 1,200, 1,300, 1,400, 1,500, 1,600, 1,700, 1,800, 1,900, 2,000

Page 48

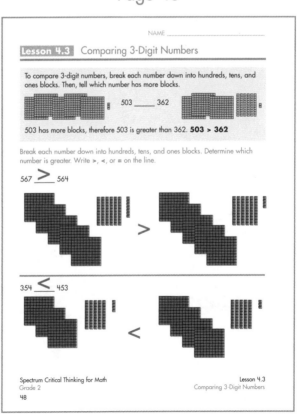

Lesson 4.3 Comparing 3-Digit Numbers

To compare 3-digit numbers, break each number down into hundreds, tens, and ones blocks. Then, tell which number has more blocks.

503 _____ 362

503 has more blocks, therefore 503 is greater than 362. **503 > 362**

Break each number down into hundreds, tens, and ones blocks. Determine which number is greater. Write >, <, or = on the line.

567 **>** 564

>

354 **<** 453

<

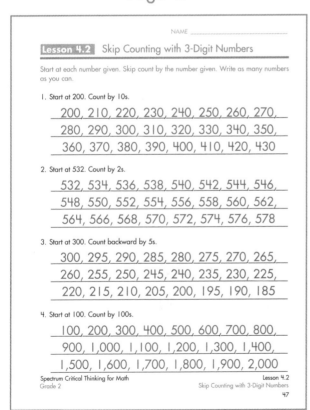

113

Answer Key

Page 49

NAME _____

Lesson 4.3 Comparing 3-Digit Numbers

When comparing 3-digit numbers, you can use a number line to help you tell which number is greater and which one is smaller.

122 _____ 245

122 +100 222 +10 +10 242 245

The number to the left on the number line is always less than the number on the right. Therefore, 122 is less than 245. **122 < 245**

Show each number given on a number line. Determine which number is greater. Write >, <, or = on the line.

148 **<** 369

148 +100 248 +100 348 +10 358 +10 368 +1 369

959 **>** 767

+100 +10 +10 +10 +10 +10 +10 +10 +10 +10 +1
767 867 959

Page 50

NAME _____

Lesson 4.4 Adding 3-Digit Numbers

You can combine hundreds, tens, and ones blocks to help you add 3-digit numbers.

188
+ 365

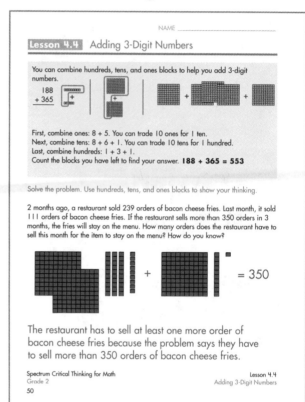

First, combine ones: 8 + 5. You can trade 10 ones for 1 ten.
Next, combine tens: 8 + 6 + 1. You can trade 10 tens for 1 hundred.
Last, combine hundreds: 1 + 3 + 1.
Count the blocks you have left to find your answer. **188 + 365 = 553**

Solve the problem. Use hundreds, tens, and ones blocks to show your thinking.

2 months ago, a restaurant sold 239 orders of bacon cheese fries. Last month, it sold 111 orders of bacon cheese fries. If the restaurant sells more than 350 orders in 3 months, the fries will stay on the menu. How many orders does the restaurant have to sell this month for the item to stay on the menu? How do you know?

= 350

The restaurant has to sell at least one more order of bacon cheese fries because the problem says they have to sell more than 350 orders of bacon cheese fries.

Page 51

NAME _____

Lesson 4.4 Adding 3-Digit Numbers

You can use a number line to solve addition problems with 3-digit numbers.

788
+ 149

100 + 40 + 9
788 +100 888 +10 +10 +10 928 937

Add. Use a number line to show your thinking.

203 + 299 =

+200
+90
+9
203 +100 +100 403 493 502

338 + 187 =

+100 +10 +10 +10 +10 +10 +10
338 438 518 525

Page 52

NAME _____

Lesson 4.5 Subtracting 3-Digit Numbers

You can use models to help you subtract 3-digit numbers.

486
− 109

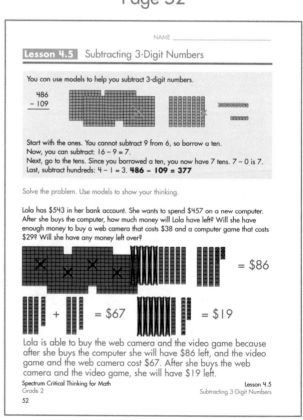

Start with the ones. You cannot subtract 9 from 6, so borrow a ten.
Now, you can subtract: 16 − 9 = 7.
Next, go to the tens. Since you borrowed a ten, you now have 7 tens. 7 − 0 is 7.
Last, subtract hundreds: 4 − 1 = 3. **486 − 109 = 377**

Solve the problem. Use models to show your thinking.

Lola has $543 in her bank account. She wants to spend $457 on a new computer. After she buys the computer, how much money will Lola have left? Will she have enough money to buy a web camera that costs $38 and a computer game that costs $29? Will she have any money left over?

= $86

+ = $67 = $19

Lola is able to buy the web camera and the video game because after she buys the computer she will have $86 left, and the video game and the web camera cost $67. After she buys the web camera and the video game, she will have $19 left.

Page 53

Lesson 4.5 Subtracting 3-Digit Numbers

You can use a number line to subtract 3-digit numbers.

519
− 120

Start your number line with the number you are subtracting from.
First, count backward by the hundreds (100).
Next, count backward by the tens (20).
Last, count backward by the ones (0).
The number you land on is your answer. **519 − 120 = 399**

Subtract. Use a number line to show your thinking.

710 − 447 =

(263)   270   310   710

Write the subtraction problem shown on the number line.

$119 - 104 = 15$

Page 54

Lesson 4.6 Creating 3-Digit Problems

The answer is:	The questions might be:
675	553 + 122
	794 − 119
	230 + 445

Write 3 problems for each answer given.

812

Students' answers will vary.

305

Students' answers will vary.

664

Students' answers will vary.

Page 55

Lesson 4.7 3-Digit Numbers in the Real World

Yasmin collected 325 bottle caps for her art project. Her school donated 299 more bottle caps. Yasmin needs 800 bottle caps to complete her project. Will she have enough to complete her project? If not, how many more bottle caps does she need?

First, you must determine how many bottle caps she has: 325 + 299 = 624. Now, you know she does **not** have enough bottle caps because 624 < 800. To find out how many more bottle caps she needs you must subtract: 800 − 624 = 176. Yasmin needs 176 more bottle caps to finish her art project.

Solve the problem. Explain your thinking.

Roxanne makes jewelry to sell at craft fairs. She has 251 red beads and 439 blue beads in her kit. To be successful at her next craft fair, she needs 900 of each color bead. How many more red beads does she need to buy?

(649) 650   700   900

How many more blue beads does she need to buy?

(461)   470   500   900

How many total beads does she need to buy before her next craft fair?

Roxanne will need to buy 649 more red beads and 461 more blue beads.

Roxanne will need to buy 1,110 total beads before her next craft fair.

Page 56

Lesson 4.7 3-Digit Numbers in the Real World

Write a word problem to go with each addition or subtraction problem. Then, solve each problem.

411 + 120 =

411
+ 120
531

Word problems will vary.

719 − 532 =

719
− 532
187

Word problems will vary.

Answer Key

Page 57

NAME _____

Check What You Learned

Working with 3-Digit Numbers

Complete the following with the number **674**.

1. Show the number in hundreds, tens, and ones blocks.

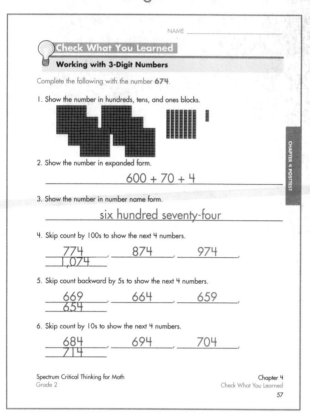

2. Show the number in expanded form.

$$600 + 70 + 4$$

3. Show the number in number name form.

six hundred seventy-four

4. Skip count by 100s to show the next 4 numbers.

774 , 874 , 974 ,
1,074

5. Skip count backward by 5s to show the next 4 numbers.

669 , 664 , 659
654

6. Skip count by 10s to show the next 4 numbers.

684 , 694 , 704
714

Spectrum Critical Thinking for Math
Grade 2

Chapter 4
Check What You Learned
57

Page 58

NAME _____

Check What You Learned

Working with 3-Digit Numbers

Compare: 226 __<__ 298

7. Use blocks.   8. Use a number line.

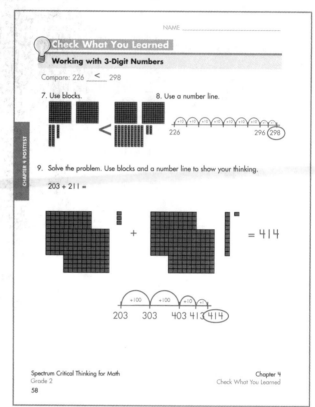

9. Solve the problem. Use blocks and a number line to show your thinking.

203 + 211 =

$$= 414$$

203   303   403 413 414

Spectrum Critical Thinking for Math
Grade 2
58

Chapter 4
Check What You Learned

Page 59

NAME _____

Check What You Know

Measurement

1. Melissa got home from swimming at 3:00 P.M. It takes her 20 minutes to walk home. What time did Melissa leave the pool? Show the time on both clocks below.

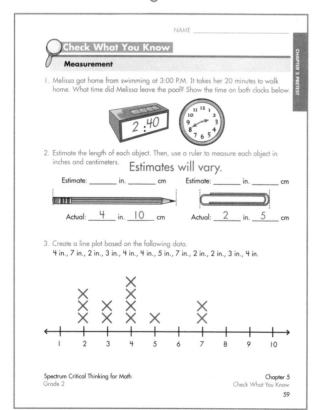

2:40

2. Estimate the length of each object. Then, use a ruler to measure each object in inches and centimeters. **Estimates will vary.**

Estimate: _____ in. _____ cm   Estimate: _____ in. _____ cm

Actual: __4__ in. __10__ cm   Actual: __2__ in. __5__ cm

3. Create a line plot based on the following data.
4 in., 7 in., 2 in., 3 in., 4 in., 4 in., 5 in., 7 in., 2 in., 2 in., 3 in., 4 in.

Spectrum Critical Thinking for Math
Grade 2

Chapter 5
Check What You Know
59

Page 60

NAME _____

Check What You Know

Measurement

Favorite Ice Cream Flavors

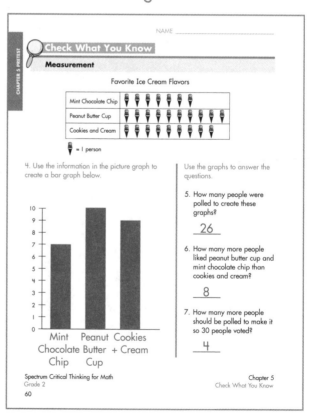

= 1 person

4. Use the information in the picture graph to create a bar graph below.

Use the graphs to answer the questions.

5. How many people were polled to create these graphs?

__26__

6. How many more people liked peanut butter cup and mint chocolate chip than cookies and cream?

__8__

7. How many more people should be polled to make it so 30 people voted?

__4__

Spectrum Critical Thinking for Math
Grade 2
60

Chapter 5
Check What You Know

Answer Key

Page 61

Page 62

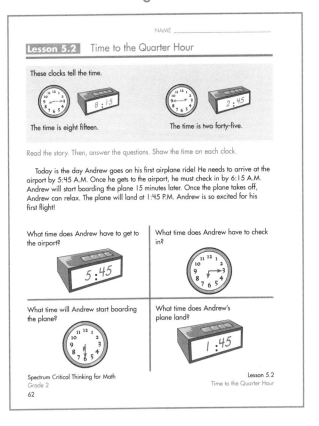

Page 63

NAME _____

Lesson 5.3 Time in the Real World

Each number on the clock represents 5 minutes of time.

From 12 to 1 is 5 minutes.
From 12 to 3 is 15 minutes.
From 12 to 6 is 30 minutes.
From 12 to 9 is 45 minutes.
From 12 to 12 is 60 minutes (1 hour).

Solve. Write the time on each clock given.

Kennedy went for a walk at 4:30 P.M. She walked 15 minutes down the road. What time did Kennedy stop walking?

4:45

Frederico turned off the television at 6:00 P.M. He had watched TV for 25 minutes before he turned it off. What time did Frederico start watching TV?

5:35

Spectrum Critical Thinking for Math
Grade 2

Lesson 5.3
Time in the Real World
63

Page 64

NAME _____

Lesson 5.4 Estimating Inches

To estimate the length of an object, use what you already know about measurement to make your best guess at how long the object is. The word **about** is used to describe how long the object might be.

| inches | 1 | 2 | 3 | 4 | 5 | 6 |

The paper clip is about 1 inch long.

Use the ruler above to estimate how many inches long each object is.

about ___6___ inches

about ___3___ inches

about ___5___ inches

Spectrum Critical Thinking for Math
Grade 2

Lesson 5.4
Estimating Inches
64

Answer Key

Page 65

Lesson 5.5 Estimating Centimeters

The safety pin is about 2 centimeters long.

Use the ruler above to estimate how many centimeters long each object is.

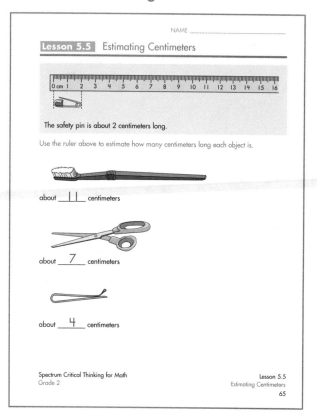

about __11__ centimeters

about __7__ centimeters

about __4__ centimeters

Page 66

Lesson 5.6 Measuring Inches

To measure an object to the nearest inch, line up the edge of the ruler with the end of the object you are measuring. Look to the right. To determine the nearest inch, look to see what number the right end is closest to.

To the nearest inch, the nail is 2 inches long.

Choose 5 different writing tools (pen, pencil, crayon, marker, highlighter, etc.). Use a ruler to measure each tool to the nearest inch. Write the name and length of the tool on the lines below.

1. <u>Students' answers will vary.</u>   _____ inch(es)

2. <u>Students' answers will vary.</u>   _____ inch(es)

3. <u>Students' answers will vary.</u>   _____ inch(es)

4. <u>Students' answers will vary.</u>   _____ inch(es)

5. <u>Students' answers will vary.</u>   _____ inch(es)

Page 67

Lesson 5.7 Measuring Centimeters

Measure centimeters the same way you measure inches.

The tweezers are 8 centimeters long.

Use a ruler to measure each object in centimeters.

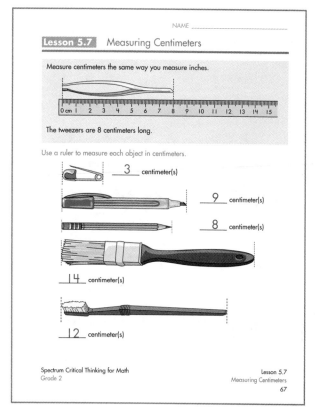

__3__ centimeter(s)

__9__ centimeter(s)

__8__ centimeter(s)

__14__ centimeter(s)

__12__ centimeter(s)

Page 68

Lesson 5.8 Comparing Measurements

You can compare measurements in inches and centimeters.

The toothbrush is 12 centimeters long.
The toothbrush is about 5 inches long.

Choose 5 eating utensils (fork, spoon, knife, chopstick, spork, etc.). Ask an adult to help you with any sharp utensils! Use a ruler to measure each in centimeters. Then, measure again to the nearest inch. Write the name of the utensil and how long it is on the lines below.

1. <u>Students' answers will vary.</u> ____ inches ____ centimeters

2. <u>Students' answers will vary.</u> ____ inches ____ centimeters

3. <u>Students' answers will vary.</u> ____ inches ____ centimeters

4. <u>Students' answers will vary.</u> ____ inches ____ centimeters

5. <u>Students' answers will vary.</u> ____ inches ____ centimeters

What do you notice about the measurements in centimeters compared to those in inches? What explains this?

<u>Centimeters are always a larger number compared to inches. Centimeter is a smaller unit of measurement, so it needs more to equal 1 inch.</u>

Answer Key

Page 69

NAME _____

Lesson 5.9 Measurement in the Real World

You can use a number line to help you solve word problems involving lengths.

Becca wants to make a 28-inch necklace out of ribbon. She has a piece of ribbon that is 45 inches long. How many inches does Becca need to cut off in order to make her necklace the correct length?

Start at 45 and count backward until you reach 28.
The number you counted is the amount Becca needs to cut off: 17 inches.

Solve. Use a number line to show your work.

Blake lines up 4 of her pencils and measures them. The total length of Blake's pencils is 60 centimeters. Delinda lines up 3 of her pencils and measures them. The total length of Delinda's pencils is 30 centimeters. What is the total length of all of Blake and Delinda's pencils?

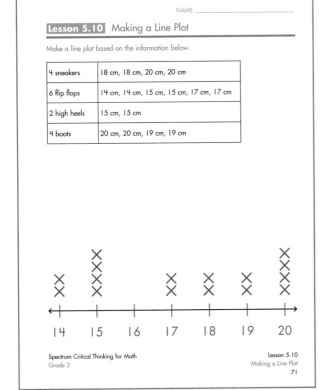

The total length of Blake and Delinda's pencils is 90 inches.

Page 70

NAME _____

Lesson 5.10 Making a Line Plot

A line plot is a simple way to organize small amounts of data along a number line. After you draw the number line and write what numbers you will use, plot X's above each number to show each piece of data.

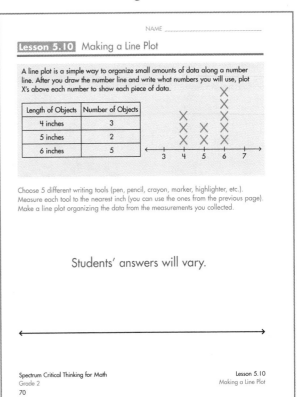

Length of Objects	Number of Objects
4 inches	3
5 inches	2
6 inches	5

Choose 5 different writing tools (pen, pencil, crayon, marker, highlighter, etc.). Measure each tool to the nearest inch (you can use the ones from the previous page). Make a line plot organizing the data from the measurements you collected.

Students' answers will vary.

Page 71

NAME _____

Lesson 5.10 Making a Line Plot

Make a line plot based on the information below.

4 sneakers	18 cm, 18 cm, 20 cm, 20 cm
6 flip flops	14 cm, 14 cm, 15 cm, 15 cm, 17 cm, 17 cm
2 high heels	15 cm, 15 cm
4 boots	20 cm, 20 cm, 19 cm, 19 cm

Page 72

NAME _____

Lesson 5.10 Making a Line Plot

Create a line plot using the length of each side of each shape.

119

Answer Key

Page 73

NAME

Lesson 5.10 Making a Line Plot

Create a line plot based on the measurements given below.

_7_ centimeters

_10_ centimeters

_10_ centimeters

_10_ centimeters

_5_ centimeters

X X X
at 5, 7, and two at 10 plus one more

1 2 3 4 5 6 7 8 9 10 11 12 13 14 15

Page 74

NAME

Lesson 5.11 Reading Picture Graphs

Ella asked her neighborhood friends about their pets. She made this picture graph to show the results. One animal picture means one pet.

OUR PETS

Dog	🐕🐕🐕🐕🐕
Cat	🐈🐈🐈🐈🐈🐈🐈
Fish	🐟🐟🐟🐟🐟
Turtle	🐢🐢
None	IIII

Use the picture graph to answer the questions.

How many pets do Ella's neighborhood friends have?

21

How many more fish and turtles are there than dogs?

1 more

Which animal is most popular?

Cats are most popular.

Page 75

NAME

Lesson 5.12 Creating Picture Graphs

Lamar looked around his house and counted the shapes of different objects. He wanted to create a picture graph to show his results.

Use the following clues to complete the picture graph.

- The fewest objects were shaped like a circle.
- 1 more object was shaped like a triangle than a circle.
- 2 fewer objects were shaped like a triangle than a square.
- 6 objects were shaped like a circle.
- 3 more objects were shaped like a star than a triangle.

Shapes Around the House

Triangles	▲▲▲▲▲▲▲
Stars	★★★★★★★★★★
Squares	■■■■■■■■■
Circles	●●●●●●

Answer the questions based on the data from the picture graph.

How many objects are there in all?

32

How many more stars than triangles are there?

3

Page 76

NAME

Lesson 5.13 Reading Bar Graphs

A total of 4 Walker Wildcats players scored in the basketball game last week. The points each player scored are shown in the bar graph.

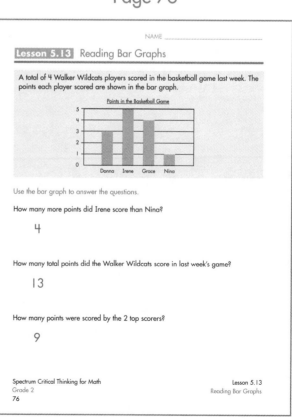

Points in the Basketball Game

Use the bar graph to answer the questions.

How many more points did Irene score than Nina?

4

How many total points did the Walker Wildcats score in last week's game?

13

How many points were scored by the 2 top scorers?

9

Answer Key

Page 77

NAME _____

Lesson 5.14 Creating Bar Graphs

The members of a book club voted for their favorite fruits. They wanted to create a bar graph to show the results.

Use the following clues to complete the bar graph.

- The same amount of people chose apples, bananas, and pears.
- Grapes had the least number of votes.
- Apples had 2 fewer votes than oranges.
- Oranges got 6 votes.
- Grapes had more than 2 votes.

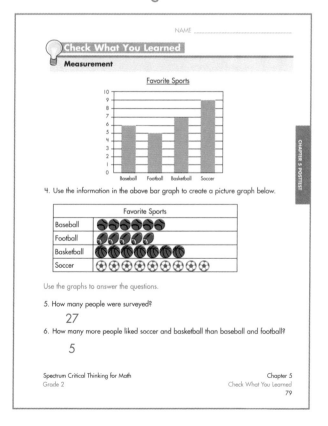

Our Favorite Fruits

Answer the questions based on the data from the bar graph.

How many people are in the book club?

21

How many people voted for grapes and apples?

7

Page 78

NAME _____

Check What You Learned

Measurement

1. Estimate the length of the paper clip. Then, use a ruler to measure the paper clip in inches and centimeters. Estimates will vary.

Estimate: _____ in. _____ cm

Actual: __1.5__ in. __4__ cm

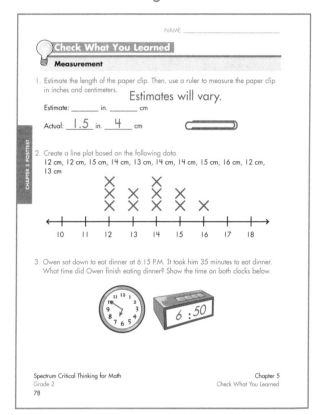

2. Create a line plot based on the following data.
12 cm, 12 cm, 15 cm, 14 cm, 13 cm, 14 cm, 14 cm, 15 cm, 16 cm, 12 cm, 13 cm

3. Owen sat down to eat dinner at 6:15 P.M. It took him 35 minutes to eat dinner. What time did Owen finish eating dinner? Show the time on both clocks below.

6 : 50

Page 79

NAME _____

Check What You Learned

Measurement

Favorite Sports

4. Use the information in the above bar graph to create a picture graph below.

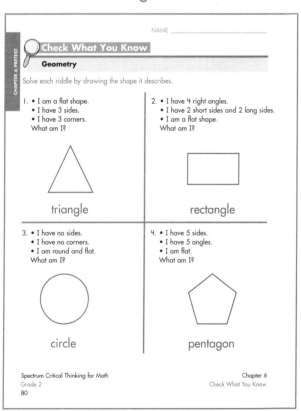

Favorite Sports	
Baseball	
Football	
Basketball	
Soccer	

Use the graphs to answer the questions.

5. How many people were surveyed?
27

6. How many more people liked soccer and basketball than baseball and football?
5

Page 80

NAME _____

Check What You Know

Geometry

Solve each riddle by drawing the shape it describes.

1. • I am a flat shape.
   • I have 3 sides.
   • I have 3 corners.
   What am I?

   triangle

2. • I have 4 right angles.
   • I have 2 short sides and 2 long sides.
   • I am a flat shape.
   What am I?

   rectangle

3. • I have no sides.
   • I have no corners.
   • I am round and flat.
   What am I?

   circle

4. • I have 5 sides.
   • I have 5 angles.
   • I am flat.
   What am I?

   pentagon

Answer Key

Page 81

NAME _____

Check What You Know
Geometry

CHAPTER 6 PRETEST

5. At her birthday party, Tara received several gifts. One gift was in a box that had faces shaped like squares. The box had 6 faces and was wrapped in pretty green paper. What shape is the box? Draw the shape below.

cube

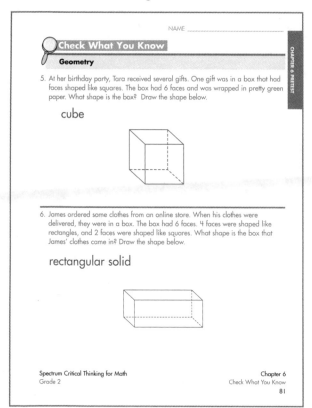

6. James ordered some clothes from an online store. When his clothes were delivered, they were in a box. The box had 6 faces. 4 faces were shaped like rectangles, and 2 faces were shaped like squares. What shape is the box that James' clothes came in? Draw the shape below.

rectangular solid

Spectrum Critical Thinking for Math
Grade 2

Chapter 6
Check What You Know
81

Page 82

NAME _____

Lesson 6.1 Attributes of Plane Shapes

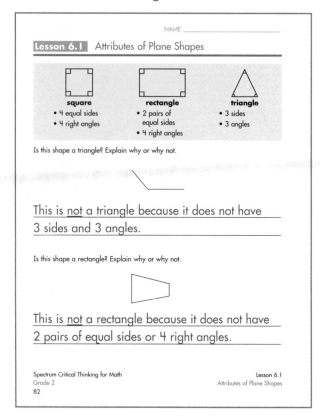

square	rectangle	triangle
• 4 equal sides	• 2 pairs of equal sides	• 3 sides
• 4 right angles	• 4 right angles	• 3 angles

Is this shape a triangle? Explain why or why not.

This is not a triangle because it does not have 3 sides and 3 angles.

Is this shape a rectangle? Explain why or why not.

This is not a rectangle because it does not have 2 pairs of equal sides or 4 right angles.

Spectrum Critical Thinking for Math
Grade 2
82

Lesson 6.1
Attributes of Plane Shapes

Page 83

NAME _____

Lesson 6.1 Attributes of Plane Shapes

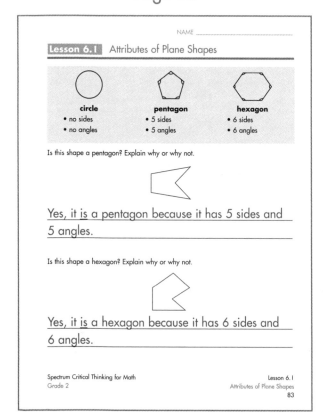

circle	pentagon	hexagon
• no sides	• 5 sides	• 6 sides
• no angles	• 5 angles	• 6 angles

Is this shape a pentagon? Explain why or why not.

Yes, it is a pentagon because it has 5 sides and 5 angles.

Is this shape a hexagon? Explain why or why not.

Yes, it is a hexagon because it has 6 sides and 6 angles.

Spectrum Critical Thinking for Math
Grade 2

Lesson 6.1
Attributes of Plane Shapes
83

Page 84

NAME _____

Lesson 6.2 Attributes of Solid Shapes

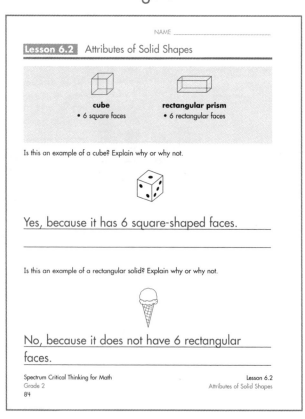

cube	rectangular prism
• 6 square faces	• 6 rectangular faces

Is this an example of a cube? Explain why or why not.

Yes, because it has 6 square-shaped faces.

Is this an example of a rectangular solid? Explain why or why not.

No, because it does not have 6 rectangular faces.

Spectrum Critical Thinking for Math
Grade 2
84

Lesson 6.2
Attributes of Solid Shapes

Answer Key

Page 85

Lesson 6.2 Attributes of Solid Shapes

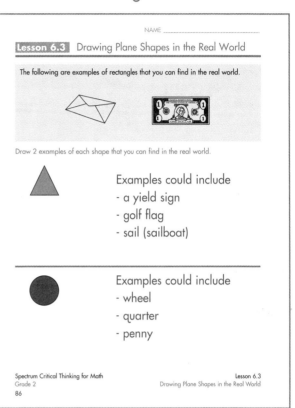

square pyramid
- 4 triangular faces
- 1 square face

sphere
- no faces
- perfectly round

Lucy says this beach ball is an example of a sphere. Is she correct? Explain why or why not.

Yes, because it has no faces and is perfectly round.

Tony tells his friends that his soup can is the shape of a square pyramid. Is Tony correct? Explain why or why not.

The soup can is <u>not</u> a square pyramid. It does not have any triangular faces or square faces.

Page 86

Lesson 6.3 Drawing Plane Shapes in the Real World

The following are examples of rectangles that you can find in the real world.

Draw 2 examples of each shape that you can find in the real world.

 Examples could include
- a yield sign
- golf flag
- sail (sailboat)

 Examples could include
- wheel
- quarter
- penny

Page 87

Lesson 6.4 Drawing Plane Shapes

This pattern is an A-B-C pattern:

A B C A B C A B C A B C A B C

This pattern is an A-A-B pattern:

A A B A A B A A B A A B A A B

Create two different patterns using plane shapes only. Repeat and draw each pattern 3 times. Label your patterns.

Answers will vary.

Page 88

Lesson 6.5 Drawing Solid Shapes in the Real World

The following are examples of a cylinder that you can find in the real world.

Draw 2 examples of each shape that you can find in the real world.

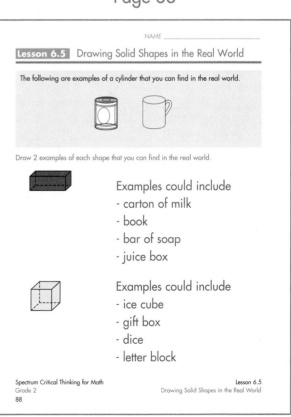 Examples could include
- carton of milk
- book
- bar of soap
- juice box

Examples could include
- ice cube
- gift box
- dice
- letter block

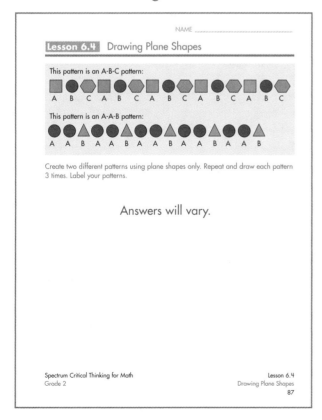

Page 89

NAME _____

Lesson 6.6 Drawing Solid Shapes

This pattern is an A-B-C-C pattern:

A B C C A B C C A B C C

Create two different patterns using solid shapes only. Repeat and draw each pattern 3 times. Label your patterns.

Answers will vary.

Page 90

NAME _____

Check What You Learned

Geometry

1. Denise was cutting out shapes to make a shape collage. She cut out a shape that had 4 sides. Each side was a different length and the corners were not all right angles. Denise told her friend that this shape was a rectangle. Her friend was unsure. Is this shape a rectangle? Explain why or why not.

No, this is <u>not</u> a rectangle because to be a rectangle 2 pairs of sides must be equal and all the corners must be right angles.

2. The Lopez family is moving across the country. They are packing up everything in large and small boxes. Amy Lopez starts packing a box with 6 square faces. Fernando Lopez starts packing a box with 6 rectangular faces. Mr. Lopez says they are packing two different boxes, but Amy and Fernando say they are the same. Are the boxes the same? Explain why or why not.

The boxes are <u>not</u> the same. Amy is packing a cube because it has square faces. Fernando is packing a rectangular solid because it has rectangular faces.

Page 91

NAME _____

Check What You Learned

Geometry

3. Brady did a shape walk around his house. He counted how many of each shape he saw in his house. Then, he organized the information in a tally chart. Use the tally chart to create a picture graph of shapes.

Shape	Number of Shapes
square pyramid	II
cube	̶I̶H̶T̶ I
triangle	IIII
pentagon	III
hexagon	III

Shapes in Brady's House

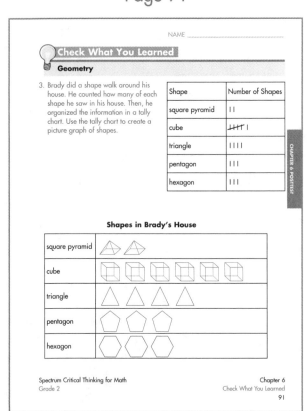

square pyramid	△ △
cube	▱ ▱ ▱ ▱ ▱ ▱
triangle	△ △ △ △
pentagon	⬠ ⬠ ⬠
hexagon	⬡ ⬡ ⬡

Page 92

NAME _____

Check What You Know

Parts of a Whole

1. Show 2 different ways to partition a rectangle in half.

2. Quinn divides his rectangular suitcase into 4 sections so he can pack shorts, shirts, pants, and pajamas for his trip. Show 2 different ways Quinn can divide his suitcase. Shade the section where he should pack pajamas in both drawings.

3. Vanessa bought a giant chocolate chip cookie for her mother's birthday. She cut the cookie into thirds and gave her mom $\frac{1}{3}$. Show 2 different ways Vanessa could have divided the cookie. Shade the piece she gave to her mom in both drawings.

Answer Key

Page 93

NAME _____

Lesson 7.1 Partitioning Rectangles in the Real World

Chelsea ordered a rectangular pizza. She cut the pizza into fourths and ate $\frac{1}{4}$ of the pizza for lunch:

Here is another way Chelsea could have cut the pizza and eaten $\frac{1}{4}$ of the pizza:

Jasper has a garden shaped like a rectangle. He divides his garden into fourths so he can plant corn, potatoes, carrots, and squash. Show 2 ways Jasper could divide up his garden. Then, shade where he should plant the squash.

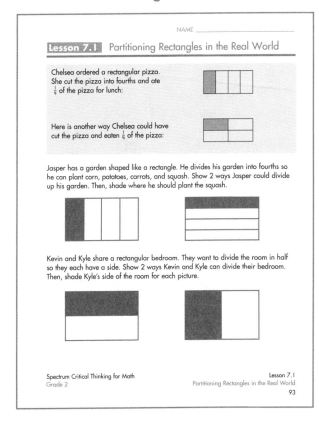

Kevin and Kyle share a rectangular bedroom. They want to divide the room in half so they each have a side. Show 2 ways Kevin and Kyle can divide their bedroom. Then, shade Kyle's side of the room for each picture.

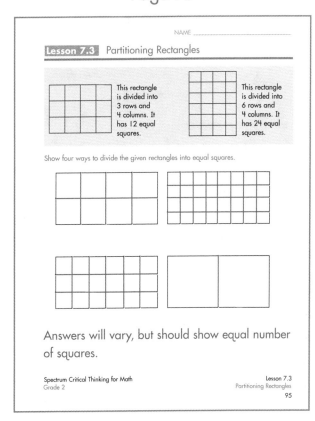

Spectrum Critical Thinking for Math
Grade 2

Lesson 7.1
Partitioning Rectangles in the Real World
93

Page 94

NAME _____

Lesson 7.2 Partitioning Circles in the Real World

Myra baked a circular apple pie. She cut the pie into thirds and ate $\frac{1}{3}$ of the pie:

Here is another way Myra could have cut the pie and eaten $\frac{1}{3}$ of it:

Luke made a circle-shaped cheese pizza for lunch. He divided the pizza into thirds and gave $\frac{1}{3}$ to his little brother. Show 2 ways Luke could divide the cheese pizza. Then, shade the part that Luke's little brother ate in both drawings.

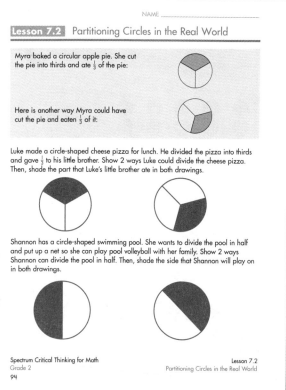

Shannon has a circle-shaped swimming pool. She wants to divide the pool in half and put up a net so she can play pool volleyball with her family. Show 2 ways Shannon can divide the pool in half. Then, shade the side that Shannon will play on in both drawings.

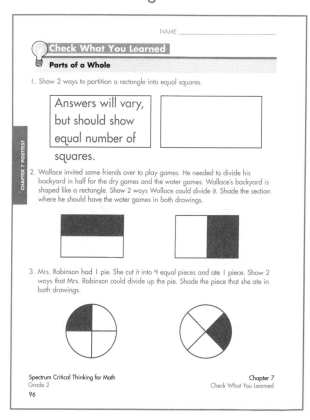

Spectrum Critical Thinking for Math
Grade 2
94

Lesson 7.2
Partitioning Circles in the Real World

Page 95

NAME _____

Lesson 7.3 Partitioning Rectangles

This rectangle is divided into 3 rows and 4 columns. It has 12 equal squares.

This rectangle is divided into 6 rows and 4 columns. It has 24 equal squares.

Show four ways to divide the given rectangles into equal squares.

Answers will vary, but should show equal number of squares.

Spectrum Critical Thinking for Math
Grade 2

Lesson 7.3
Partitioning Rectangles
95

Page 96

NAME _____

💡 **Check What You Learned**

Parts of a Whole

1. Show 2 ways to partition a rectangle into equal squares.

Answers will vary, but should show equal number of squares.

2. Wallace invited some friends over to play games. He needed to divide his backyard in half for the dry games and the water games. Wallace's backyard is shaped like a rectangle. Show 2 ways Wallace could divide it. Shade the section where he should have the water games in both drawings.

3. Mrs. Robinson had 1 pie. She cut it into 4 equal pieces and ate 1 piece. Show 2 ways that Mrs. Robinson could divide up the pie. Shade the piece that she ate in both drawings.

CHAPTER 7 POSTTEST

Spectrum Critical Thinking for Math
Grade 2
96

Chapter 7
Check What You Learned

Page 97

NAME _____

Final Test Chapters 1-7

1. Draw an array to show the equation. Then, solve the equation. Circle whether the total is even or odd.

$3 + 3 + 3 + 3 + 3 =$

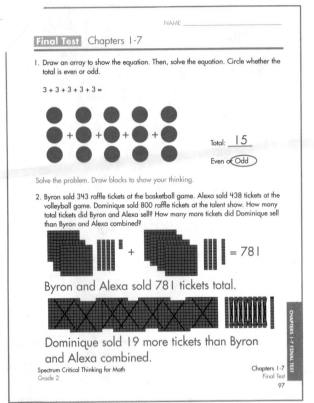

Total: _15_

Even or (Odd)

Solve the problem. Draw blocks to show your thinking.

2. Byron sold 343 raffle tickets at the basketball game. Alexa sold 438 tickets at the volleyball game. Dominique sold 800 raffle tickets at the talent show. How many total tickets did Byron and Alexa sell? How many more tickets did Dominique sell than Byron and Alexa combined?

= 781

Byron and Alexa sold 781 tickets total.

Dominique sold 19 more tickets than Byron and Alexa combined.

Spectrum Critical Thinking for Math
Grade 2

Chapters 1-7
Final Test
97

Page 98

NAME _____

Final Test Chapters 1-7

Solve. Use a number line to show your thinking.

Fiona is making a flower arrangement for her grandmother. She uses 5 white daisies, 5 pink daisies, 6 red roses, and 6 yellow roses.

3. How many daisies does Fiona use?

Fiona has 10 daisies.

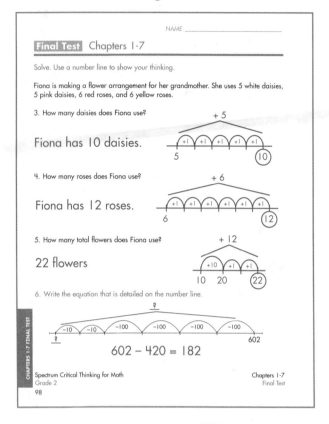

4. How many roses does Fiona use?

Fiona has 12 roses.

5. How many total flowers does Fiona use?

22 flowers

6. Write the equation that is detailed on the number line.

$602 - 420 = 182$

Spectrum Critical Thinking for Math
Grade 2
98

Chapters 1-7
Final Test

Page 99

NAME _____

Final Test Chapters 1-7

Work with the number **378** in the following ways:

7. Write using number name.

three hundred seventy-eight

8. Write using expanded form.

$300 + 70 + 8$

9. Compare 378 to 482 using blocks.

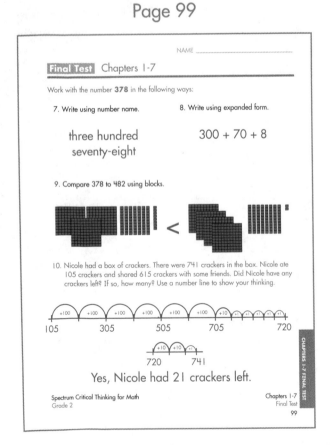

$<$

10. Nicole had a box of crackers. There were 741 crackers in the box. Nicole ate 105 crackers and shared 615 crackers with some friends. Did Nicole have any crackers left? If so, how many? Use a number line to show your thinking.

Yes, Nicole had 21 crackers left.

Spectrum Critical Thinking for Math
Grade 2

Chapters 1-7
Final Test
99

Page 100

NAME _____

Final Test Chapters 1-7

11. Estimate the length of each object. Then, use a ruler to measure each object to the nearest inch and nearest centimeter.

Estimates will vary.

Estimate: _____ in. _____ cm   Estimate: _____ in. _____ cm

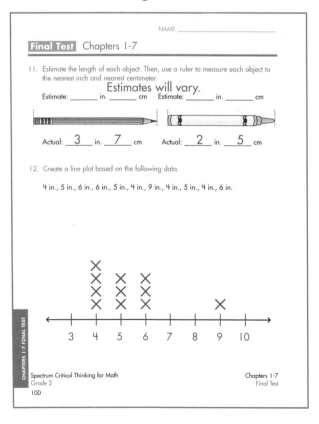

Actual: _3_ in. _7_ cm   Actual: _2_ in. _5_ cm

12. Create a line plot based on the following data.

4 in., 5 in., 6 in., 6 in., 5 in., 4 in., 9 in., 4 in., 5 in., 4 in., 6 in.

Spectrum Critical Thinking for Math
Grade 2
100

Chapters 1-7
Final Test